"Yay!" said Hannah. "I love to paint!" She ran up the last two steps, opened the gate in the lattice-work fence, and ran over to the garage.

Hannah took the brush out of the can of yellow paint, wiped the paint off on the edge of the can so it wouldn't drip, and painted one of the two unpainted shingles her father had saved for her. The paint was smooth and glossy. She painted slowly and carefully. Then she put the brush into the can of turpentine, took the other brush out of the can of blue paint, and painted the shingle next to the yellow one blue. When she finished, she put that brush into the can of turpentine too, and she closed both cans of paint.

"Good!" said her father. "Those are the two best-looking shingles of all!"

You're the Best, Hannah!

You're the Best, Hannah!

by
Mindy Warshaw Skolsky

Illustrated by Patrick Faricy

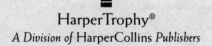

HarperTrophy®
A Division of HarperCollins Publishers

You're the Best, Hannah!

Text copyright © 2000 by Mindy Warshaw Skolsky

Illustrations copyright © 2000 by Patrick Faricy

Library of Congress Cataloging-in-Publication Data

Skolsky, Mindy Warshaw.

 [Hannah and the best father on route 9W]

 You're the best, Hannah! / by Mindy Warshaw Skolsky , illustrated by Patrick Faricy.

  p.   cm.

 Summary: In the 1930's at their family restaurant in rural New York state, Hannah and
her father each enter separate contests and help each other through the ups and downs of
competing.

  ISBN 0-06-440846-9 (pbk.)

 [1. Contests—Fiction.   2. Fathers and Daughters—Fiction.   3. Restaurants—Fiction.
4. Dogs—Fiction.   5. Family life—New York (State)—Fiction.   6. New York (State)—
Fiction.]   I. Faricy, Patrick, ill.   II. Title

PZ7.S62836 Yo 2000   99-47110

[Fic]—dc21   CIP

                                                                             AC

First Harper Trophy edition, 2000

Originally published as *Hannah and the Best Father on Route 9W* by Harper & Row, 1982

Visit us on the World Wide Web!

www.harperchildrens.com

To Trudy and Gene
and my sister Eileen
and Ada L.
with love

Fairy Tales
and Matzo Balls

Hannah sat in her secret place at the top of the mountain and looked down at the Hudson River. Her dog, Skippy, sat beside her.

"Isn't it beautiful up here, Skippy?" asked Hannah. Her legs hung down over the edge of the mountain, and she swung her feet. Skippy thumped his tail on the ground.

They turned their heads at the same time and looked at each other, nose to nose.

"Oh, I'm *so* glad you're my dog," said Hannah. She thought of the day last year when customers had driven off from The Grand View Restaurant and left a little, skinny, shivering puppy behind. The customers had never come back. Hannah had hugged the puppy till it stopped shivering and she had fed it and cared for it till it wasn't little and skinny anymore.

"You're so big now!" said Hannah. "I used to carry you up here in my pocket! Now you run up here every day with me to my secret place and you race me down the mountain so fast! And you run up here by yourself now too, and I have to call and *call* you to come home!"

Skippy licked Hannah's nose.

Hannah fell back onto the ground and looked up at the sky through the branches of a tall tree. She saw layers of branches and twigs filled with fat yellow-green buds. Some of the buds had burst open, and Hannah thought it looked like yellow-green lace popping out of them. She sat back up and looked down at the sun spots sparkling all the way across the river over to the mountain on the other side.

"Oh, spring is really the best time of the year, Skippy!" she said. "And this is my favorite place in the world. I could sit up here and just look and think about things forever." She held up her wrist and looked at her Mickey Mouse watch.

"But it's twenty to eleven!" she said. "We have to go this minute or we'll be late for *Let's Pretend!*"

Hannah jumped up. Skippy jumped up. Hannah pushed through the high grass that separated the secret place from the mountain road. Skippy followed.

"Race you down the mountain road!" said Hannah. "Last one down is a rotten egg!"

Near the bottom of the mountain road, Hannah stopped.

"You're the rotten egg, Skippy!" she said. "I won!"

But when Hannah turned around, Skippy wasn't there. Hannah could just see his tail disappearing up the mountain road.

"Skippy—*no!*" yelled Hannah. "I haven't got time to race you back up now. It's a quarter to eleven. Come *back*—or you'll miss the beginning again!"

Skippy kept running up.

"Oh, what'll I do?" said Hannah. "It's my favorite one today!"

She looked both ways and crossed Route 9W. She looked back up at the mountain.

"I'll meet you back home, Skippy!" she called. "I can't be late!"

Then she ran down 9W until she saw the sign on the roof that said:

HUNGRY? THIRSTY?
STOP HERE.
THE GRAND VIEW RESTAURANT.

Hannah stopped. She wasn't hungry. She wasn't thirsty. She was home. She couldn't take her eyes off the new colors on the building: bright blue and yellow. For weeks her father had been painting the shingles the two colors so he could win a certificate for the best-looking place on Route 9W. He had finished with the restaurant and now he was working on the garage, where the two blue-and-yellow gas pumps were.

Hannah ran over to say hello to her father.

"Well, how do you like it?" asked Hannah's

father. He stopped painting a minute and leaned against the white latticework fence between the garage and the restaurant. "Does this place look like a prizewinner or does this place look like a prizewinner?"

"It looks *beautiful*," said Hannah. "But I can't talk now. I have to hurry."

"What's the hurry?" asked her father.

"It's ten of eleven. It's almost time for *Let's Pretend!*"

Hannah ran over to the restaurant, opened the door, and went inside. She left the door open for Skippy.

"Week-end Special," she read out loud from the little blackboard inside. "Roast beef and mashed potatoes, two vegetables, bread and butter. 65¢." She studied the neat handwriting a moment.

"My mother has the best handwriting in the world," thought Hannah. She picked up a piece of chalk from the bottom of the blackboard and quickly drew roast beef and mashed potatoes in the space her mother had saved for her.

"I'll draw the carrots and peas later," she said to herself.

Week-end Special
roast beef
and mashed potatoes,
two vegetables,
bread and butter.
$.65

She ran into the kitchen. Her mother was peeking into the oven of the big black cast-iron stove.

"Mmm, it smells good!" said Hannah. "I'm back! Skippy almost made me be late."

Hannah's mother looked at the clock.

"You've got time," she said. "Calm down. Catch your breath."

"But I have to get myself ready," said Hannah.

"Okay," said her mother. "You get yourself ready. And what about getting Skippy ready for the dog show at the movies this afternoon? Are you going? Remember, if you are, he'll need a bath."

"I didn't decide yet," said Hannah. Hannah only liked to think about one thing at a time. "I'll decide after *Let's Pretend*."

"I'm going out for a few minutes and work on my garden," said her mother, "*if* I can stand to look at those blue and yellow shingles!"

"It looks *pretty*," said Hannah. "I *love* it!"

"A checkered building?" asked her mother. "It makes me dizzy! I can just imagine what those judges will think of it." She put on her gardening hat. "Call me if any customers come," she said.

"Okay," said Hannah. She crossed her fingers to keep customers from coming and ran from the kitchen through the living room and into her bedroom. She took the chair from in front of her rolltop desk and dragged it into the living room. She put it in front of the radio, which was in the corner next to the door to the kitchen. Then she looked at her Mickey Mouse watch again.

"Two minutes to eleven!" she said. She ran to the other end of the living room, where there were two French doors leading out onto a little porch. Hannah opened one of the French doors and ran out past a table with a shiny yellow umbrella. From the porch she could see both sides of the latticework fence. On one side she saw her mother bending down in her hillside garden where lots of yellow daffodils were growing now. She saw her father looking down over the fence on the other side.

"No, no, no!" Hannah heard her mother call up to her father. "No, I *don't* think you should paint the fence blue and yellow too. A fence has to be white!"

Hannah looked past her father and up at the mountain.

"*Skippy!*" she called, as loud as she could. "This is your *last chance! Hurry up!*"

Hannah's mother looked up at the porch.

"Don't worry, Hannah," she said. "You know Skippy always comes home."

"But he always runs away at the wrong time and misses things!" said Hannah. "Last week he missed the whole beginning. And today's my favorite."

"Go," said Hannah's mother. "Skippy doesn't

care if he misses the beginning. You do. I'll tell him you're inside when he comes back."

Hannah ran back inside, then she turned and ran back out onto the porch again.

"Save me two shingles to paint," she called to her father over the fence. "One yellow and one blue."

Back inside the living room, Hannah crossed over to the corner with the radio and the chair in it. She opened the kitchen door as far in toward the chair and radio as it would go. It made a little triangle enclosing the radio and the chair, and Hannah squeezed herself into the triangle and sat down.

"This is my private corner," she said to herself. "Nothing else fits in here but the radio, my chair, and me." She changed the number on the dial. "And you too, Skippy, you dope!" she said. "*You* fit in here. What a time to race back up the mountain again!"

She looked at her Mickey Mouse watch. It was eleven o'clock exactly.

Snap! Hannah turned the radio on.

"Da *dum* da da da, da *dum* da da da, da *dum* da *dum* da *dum*," Hannah sang along with the music.

"Hello, boys and girls," said the announcer. "It's time for *Let's Pretend!*"

"*Let's Pretend!*" said Hannah. "*Let's Pretend!*"

She shivered and got goose bumps on her skin every time she heard it. Then she waited for the other voice.

"Hello, girls and boys, this is Nila Mack," said the other voice Hannah was waiting for.

"Hello, Nila Mack, this is Hannah!" Hannah whispered back. Her eyes were shining. "Say it's 'The Twelve Dancing Princesses.'" She held her breath.

"Today," said Nila Mack, "we are going to hear the story of 'The Twelve Dancing Princesses.'"

Hannah exhaled. She applauded. Nila Mack had announced it at the end of *Let's Pretend* last Saturday. But each Saturday, Hannah always held her breath at the beginning until she was sure Nila Mack had kept her promise from the week before. Especially if it was one of her favorites.

And "The Twelve Dancing Princesses" was Hannah's favorite fairy tale of all.

The fairy-tale music started. Hannah sat back in her chair and closed her eyes. Her toes curled up inside her shoes.

"Oh, I just can't wait another minute!" she told the radio. "Start the story!"

Underneath her eyelids, Hannah saw the twelve princesses in their bedroom, dressed in beautiful satin ball gowns of pink and lavender and gold—with elegant dancing shoes to match! She held her breath as they opened a secret trap-door in their bedroom floor and tiptoed down a secret stairway.

"Just like our trapdoor in the bathroom and the steps to our cellar," whispered Hannah.

But the princesses didn't go to a cellar. They went to a secret underground world! They rushed through groves of trees with leaves of silver and gold and diamonds. Everything sparkled and shone in the moonlight.

"Hurry!" whispered Hannah. "Hurry!"

At the edge of a lake filled with the reflections

of stars, the princesses met twelve princes in glass rowboats! They rowed across to a secret castle. Soon they were dancing and whirling around the ballroom floor. They were having a wonderful time, and Hannah was too. She could see all the colors and the flash of their jewels while she listened to the music. She felt a tingling under the hair at the back of her neck.

"Oh, Skippy!" she said. "You're missing the best part!"

The colors were all melting into each other. The music was so beautiful it made Hannah feel like getting up and dancing too. She swayed on the chair as she listened. Underneath her eyelids, Hannah was dressed in the melting colors, and she was whirling around the ballroom floor too.

All of a sudden, a voice said, "Yoo-hoo!"

Hannah opened her eyes and stopped swaying. She knew "The Twelve Dancing Princesses" by heart. Nobody said "Yoo-hoo" in "The Twelve Dancing Princesses."

But she heard it again: "Yoo-hoo!"

"A customer must be out front!" thought

Hannah. She hoped her mother or father would hear.

Hannah tried to hide herself. She took hold of the doorknob on the kitchen door and pulled it even closer to herself. That made the triangle she was sitting in get even smaller.

She didn't want to see anybody but the princesses. She didn't want to hear anything but *Let's Pretend*.

"Yoo-hoo! Where is everybody?" called the voice.

"No fair!" thought Hannah. "I wait all week for *Let's Pretend!*"

Hannah heard footsteps come through the kitchen and into the living room. She peeked out from behind the door.

Her *Aunt Becky* was standing there—right in the middle of *Let's Pretend!*

"Hannah darling!" said Aunt Becky. "Surprise!" She rushed over and pulled the door open. "Hannah darling! My favorite person in the whole wide world! I came to see The Grand View Restaurant that I didn't even see yet!" She bent down and gave Hannah such a big hug, Hannah felt like she was smothering.

Hannah jumped up so fast, her chair fell over.

She ran to the other end of the living room and out onto the porch.

"Ma, Pa—*Aunt Becky!*" Hannah called. Then she remembered her manners and ran back inside.

"Hello, Aunt Becky," she said.

Through the French doors, she heard her mother call to her father, "Stop painting those dizzy colors! *Your sister is here!*"

In a moment, Hannah's mother and father came into the living room.

"Becky!" said Hannah's mother. "Why didn't you give us a call and tell us you were coming? We would have picked you up at the bus station."

"Well, you know me," said Aunt Becky. "I don't like to make a fuss over myself. I just like to pack my knitting needles and my wool and my guess-whats in my satchel and here I am. The bus driver gave me walking directions from the corner."

"Oh," said Hannah to herself. "Everybody's

talking! Now I can't hear the princesses go back across the lake and through the trees and up the secret stairway to the secret trapdoor to their bedroom!" She picked up her chair.

"Hannah darling," said Aunt Becky, "come out from behind the door and be sociable."

"Why don't you turn the radio off, Hannah?" asked her mother. "You've heard that story a dozen times already—once for every princess!"

"But I *like* it!" said Hannah.

"Aunt Becky is *company*," said her mother.

Hannah turned the radio off. She couldn't hear anything anyway.

Aunt Becky bent down and opened her big black satchel. She reached in and pushed aside her knitting needles and several skeins of wool.

"I'll save the knitted guess-whats for later," she said.

"Good," said Hannah to herself. She didn't like Aunt Becky's knitting so much. It was always full of lumps and bumps.

"I'll start with cooking. Guess what!" said Aunt Becky. She pulled out a jar. "It's for all of you—

I made it before I went to bed last night. Chicken soup with knaydles!"

"Ugh!" said Hannah to herself. "That's even worse than knitting!" Hannah liked chicken soup, but she didn't like knaydles. Knaydles were matzo balls, or dumplings. Her grandmother made them too when Hannah went in to visit in New York City, but Hannah didn't eat them because they were soft and fluffy. Hannah didn't like soft fluffy food. She liked things that were hard and chewy and crunchy.

The grown-ups went into the kitchen. Hannah ran behind the door and put the radio back on. The princesses were asleep in their beds and twelve pairs of worn-out dancing shoes were standing at their bedsides. The king was issuing a proclamation.

"Hear ye! Hear ye!" said the king. "Any man who can solve the riddle of how my daughters wear their shoes out every night shall win the hand of one of the princesses in marriage!"

"*Hannah!*"

Hannah sighed and turned the radio off. She

went into the kitchen too. Her mother was setting the table. Aunt Becky was standing in front of the stove stirring a big spoon around and around in a pot. Steam was coming up out of the pot and soup was simmering inside of it. Matzo balls were bobbing up and down in the soup. Hannah's father was watching Aunt Becky. His eyes were shining.

"I love knaydles," he said. Hannah went over to the table and made believe she was helping her mother.

"I don't like matzo balls," she whispered in her mother's ear. "I don't want any. They're always soft and mushy. I just like things that go crunch."

"Everything in this world cannot go 'crunch,' Hannah," said her mother under her breath. "Some things are supposed to be soft and delicate. Besides, you like charlotte russes and pancakes and spaghetti. None of those are crunchy."

"But matzo balls are *fluffy*. I don't like fluffy stuff. Grandma never makes me eat hers." Hannah helped her mother put down the silverware.

"I'm not *making* you eat them," said Hannah's mother. "But make a little exception once in a

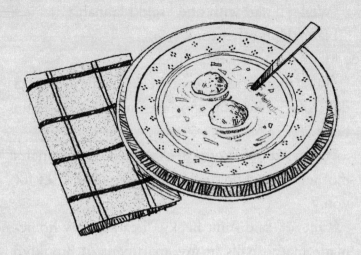

while. Especially if you know someone's feelings are hurt as easily as Aunt Becky's. Your father said something Becky didn't like two years ago, and this is the first time she's visited us since. Besides, you are Becky's favorite person in this world. What she wouldn't do for you!"

So Hannah sat down at the table and didn't tell Aunt Becky she didn't like matzo balls.

"But just give me one," she said. "One little one."

"Why only one?" asked Aunt Becky. "My knaydles are so delicious, you'll never be able to stop at one."

"Well, I'll *start* with one," said Hannah.

Hannah's mother took two.

Hannah's father took three.

"Take more," said Aunt Becky. "They're extra delicious." She put another one into his soup bowl.

"What about you, Becky?" asked Hannah's mother. "You didn't put any in the plate I set for you."

"Oh, *me!*" said Aunt Becky. "I can eat my home-made matzo balls in my apartment in Brooklyn anytime. I made these all for you. I'll just have a little sandwich later—when the roast beef is done. Eat, everybody. Eat while it's hot." She took the pot back to the stove.

Hannah's father took a bite of his matzo ball first. He started to chew and then he stopped. He had a funny expression on his face. He looked over at Hannah's mother. She was chewing now, and she had a funny expression on her face too.

Hannah took a little bite of her matzo ball. It wasn't soft and fluffy like the kind her grand-mother made. It was hard. It was *very* hard.

"Oh, it's delicious!" said Hannah.

Her mother stared at her. "You don't have to exaggerate," whispered her mother.

"But I like it," said Hannah. "It's nice and hard."

"Don't let Aunt Becky hear you say that," whispered Hannah's mother.

"Why?" asked Hannah.

"Shhh," said her mother. She ate some broth.

Hannah's father whispered, "I can't eat these! They're hard as rocks!"

Hannah's mother gave Hannah's father a little kick in the shins under the table.

"Ma!" said Hannah. "You kicked Daddy's ankle!"

"Shhh!" said Hannah's mother. "Shhh, both of you!"

Aunt Becky came back to the table.

"Where is the telephone?" she asked. "I worry about my little dog Poopala-darling when I go away from home. She has such a delicate constitution that she can't travel, and when I go away, she gets lonesome for me. So I think I'll call up my neighbor Mrs. Bluestone, who is kindly taking care of her, and say hello."

Hannah's father got up and went into the restaurant with Aunt Becky. He opened the cash register and took out some change so Aunt Becky could use the telephone booth. Then he hurried back into the kitchen.

"I can't eat these matzo balls," he said to Hannah's mother. "They're like *golf balls!* Let's get rid of them while Becky is in the phone booth."

"*I'll* get rid of them," said Hannah to her father. "I'll *eat* them. They're the hardest, crunchiest matzo balls I ever tasted."

"A matzo ball is not supposed to be hard and crunchy," said Hannah's mother.

"But I like them that way," said Hannah. She took her soupspoon, and carefully, she scooped up her mother's and father's matzo balls and put them into her bowl. She ran back into the living room and turned the radio on just in time to hear the ending of *Let's Pretend*.

"Good!" said Hannah. "I didn't miss it *all*. Now I can hear what's on next week too." Hannah liked to have all week to look forward to next Saturday.

She sat down with the bowl of soup balanced

carefully on her lap and listened to the ending of "The Twelve Dancing Princesses." One of the princesses was getting married to a nice young man who had solved the riddle of how the twelve dancing princesses wore their shoes out every night. During the wedding reception, Hannah ate her chicken soup and all the matzo balls except one.

"Oh, this is *fun*," she said to herself. "I love fairy tales and I love hard crunchy matzo balls."

"The Twelve Dancing Princesses" ended and the announcer said, "Good-bye, boys and girls. Tune in to *Let's Pretend* next week for 'Snow White and Rose Red.'"

"Hooray!" said Hannah. "That's my second favorite!"

Then the other voice Hannah always waited for said, "This is Nila Mack for *Let's Pretend* saying good-bye, girls and boys, until next Saturday."

"Good-bye, Nila Mack," Hannah whispered. "I'm sorry I had to turn it off for a while. I couldn't help it."

She sang along with the music: "Da *dum* da da

da, da *dum* da da da, da *dum,* da *dum,* da *dum,*" and she swayed on her chair again.

And just then Skippy came running into the room.

"Skippy!" said Hannah. "Where've you been so long? You missed *all* of *Let's Pretend*! You missed the *whole* 'Twelve Dancing Princesses'!" She shook her soupspoon at his nose.

Skippy jumped up and put his paws on Hannah's shoulders. He licked her face.

"Ah, that's all right," said Hannah. "I can't get mad at you. You can listen with me *next* week: 'Snow White and Rose Red.' Here—I saved you something."

And she popped the last matzo ball into Skippy's mouth.

Tips and Decisions

Hannah and Skippy sat on a little rag rug in the cellar between Hannah's father's worktable and the wooden stairway. Hannah's arm was around Skippy's neck and their heads were together.

"Oh, Skippy," said Hannah, "I know you're just trying to be friendly and say hello when you jump up on people, but I keep *telling* you—grown-ups don't like it." Skippy thumped his tail on the floor. "See, Aunt Becky never met you before, so when she came out of the phone booth and you jumped up on her, the reason she screamed was because she got *scared*," Hannah continued. "So *try* to remember not to jump up on any more grown-ups like that so you won't get sent down here so much—okay?" Skippy licked Hannah's cheek. "My mother says you have to stay in the cellar all the while Aunt Becky is here now. Oh, I *wish* you had a doghouse outside."

Skippy's eyes shone.

"I have to make up my mind what to do about the dog show now," said Hannah. "It's only at the four-o'clock movie. I could go at two o'clock the way I usually do and see just the movie without the dog show. Then I'd see the movie sooner—it's Shirley Temple, Skippy! And I wouldn't have to hear how loud my father puts the opera on the radio. But if I wait till four o'clock, I can take you with me to the dog show. But I don't know if you'd *like* to be in a dog show."

Skippy licked Hannah's arm.

"And whichever show I pick," Hannah asked, "what if those judges come to look at the restaurant while I'm gone? I don't want to miss Shirley Temple, but I don't want to miss the judges either. My mother says they don't tell you when they're coming because they want to surprise you. But my father says this is the date they came last year, so maybe this is when they'll come again."

Skippy wagged his tail.

"So *do* you want to be in a dog show, Skippy?" Hannah asked. She jumped up. Skippy jumped up. Hannah caught his front paws and she and Skippy danced around in a circle.

"I'm a dancing princess and you're a prince!" said Hannah. They sat back down in the middle of the old rag rug. Hannah leaned her head against Skippy's again.

"I wonder if they have judges at the dog show too," she said. "You should have seen the ones who came to the restaurant last year—they were so *fancy*! One lady had a funny pair of glasses with only one handle and another lady had a fur scarf with a fox's nose at the end! And there was a man with such a high stiff collar!" Hannah remembered how happy she had been when the judges had given The Grand View Restaurant the certificate for Cleanest Place on Route 9W. And she remembered how sorry she had been when they hadn't given the one for Most Attractive, because her father had been disappointed.

"Too plain to be Most Attractive," the lady with the fur scarf had said when Hannah's father had asked.

"It would need to be more spectacular to be Most Attractive," the man with the stiff collar had added.

Hannah's father had been thinking all year of ways to make The Grand View Restaurant less plain and more spectacular. He had thought of the blue-and-yellow checkerboard idea a few weeks ago and had been working as hard and as fast as he could ever since.

"I hope my father wins the certificate for Most Attractive Place on Route 9W this time, don't you?" Hannah asked. She turned her head and looked into Skippy's eyes.

"Oh, I just *love* to talk to you, Skippy," Hannah said. "I can tell you *everything*—and you listen better than anybody. So what'll I do about the movies and the dog show and the judges, though? I still can't decide—*say something!*"

Skippy licked Hannah's hand. Hannah patted Skippy's head.

"I'd like to take you to the dog show," said

Hannah. "But I'm worried about going out on the stage. Last week I finally got to lead the Pledge of Allegiance in assembly after waiting all year for my turn, and you know what happened? When I finally got out on the stage and saw all those eyes looking at me, I got so embarrassed, I almost forgot the words! I couldn't wait to get *off* the stage! Otto Zimmer was holding the flag, and afterward he teased me. Oh, I *wish* I didn't always have such a hard time making up my mind. I can never decide about *anything*!"

Just then the trapdoor at the top of the wooden steps opened.

"Look—just like in 'The Twelve Dancing Princesses,'" Hannah whispered to Skippy. She looked up and saw her mother. "Would you like a roast-beef plate on the porch with Aunt Becky and Daddy before the lunch customers come?" her mother asked.

"I'm too full of matzo balls," said Hannah. "I can't eat any more lunch."

"Did you make up your mind about the dog show?"

"I'm talking it over with Skippy."

"If you take him, we'll have to give him a bath."

Hannah covered Skippy's ears. "Don't say b-a-t-h!" she said. "He hates it!"

"Okay—let me know when you decide." The trapdoor closed.

Hannah took her hands off Skippy's ears. "I know what I'll do," she told him. "I'll call my friend Aggie Branagan and ask her if she decided which show she's going to. She called me last night to see if I was taking you and I told her I'd call back." Hannah jumped up. Skippy jumped up too. Hannah went over to the wooden stairway. Skippy walked back to the middle of the rug and curled up in a circle.

Hannah started up the inside steps that her father had built when they had first bought The Grand View Restaurant. At that time there had been no inside stairway to the cellar, so her father had invented the little trapdoor in the bathroom floor and attached a wooden stairway underneath it. Hannah liked using the inside steps better than the outside ones because they were very steep, and it was fun pushing up the trapdoor. When she had gone up enough steps to reach the trapdoor, she pushed it to make it go up. But the trapdoor didn't open.

"Use the outside steps, Hannah," she heard her mother say. "I'm in the bathroom now." When you used the bathroom, you slid a bolt across one side of the trapdoor to lock it. Then no one could come up from the cellar till you slid the bolt away. That was part of the invention.

"Okay, Ma!" said Hannah. "I didn't know you were still in there." She went back down the steps. Skippy was still curled up in a circle on the rug. His tail touched his nose.

"Have a nice nap, Skippy!" Hannah called on her way out the cellar door. "I'll see you later, as soon as I make up my mind!" She closed the door quickly and started to run up the outside steps.

As she passed the porch on the side of the building, she saw her father and Aunt Becky eating on the porch at the table with the shiny yellow umbrella.

". . . so if I win," Hannah's father was saying

to Aunt Becky, "instead of The Grand View Restaurant, I'll change the name to The Checkerboard. I'll make a new sign on the roof. I'll even paint the *sign* blue and yellow."

"Good!" said Aunt Becky. "I love to play checkers."

"Oh, don't change the name of The Grand View Restaurant," Hannah wanted to say, but just then she thought of something else.

"Did you save me two shingles?" she asked her father.

"Of course," he answered. "Don't I always save you something to paint? The two cans of paint and a can of turpentine are waiting for you next to the garage there," her father said. He pointed to the other side of the fence.

"Yay!" said Hannah. "I love to paint!" She ran up the last two steps, opened the gate in the lattice-work fence, and ran over to the garage.

"I'll call Aggie as soon as I finish," she told herself.

Hannah took the brush out of the can of yellow paint, wiped the paint off on the edge of the can so it wouldn't drip, and painted one of the two unpainted shingles her father had saved for her.

The paint was smooth and glossy. She painted slowly and carefully. Then she put the brush into the can of turpentine, took the other brush out of the can of blue paint, and painted the shingle next to the yellow one blue. She was very careful not to let the two wet colors touch and run together. When she finished, she put that brush into the can of turpentine too, and she closed both cans of paint.

"Good!" said her father. He had finished eating with Aunt Becky and had come out to join Hannah. "Those are the two best-looking shingles of all!" he added. He looked over the fence and down at the garden on the other side. "If your mother would only let me paint her birdhouse and the fence blue and yellow too, everything would be a perfect match."

Aunt Becky looked down from the porch at Hannah's mother's hillside garden. "Did you make the birdhouse too, Izzie?" she called over. "It's so pretty! It looks just like a little Grand View Restaurant!"

"I made it that way on purpose," said Hannah's

father. "It was a surprise for Mollie. It even has a little porch made out of lollipop sticks—see? I'd like to paint every other stick blue and yellow but Mollie doesn't want me to."

Hannah's mother came out on the porch in the middle of the sentence.

"If I'm not careful," she said to Aunt Becky, "your brother Izzie will paint half my yellow daffodils blue!" She looked up at the umbrella over the table. "Did you ever see a painted umbrella before?" she asked.

"What's wrong with a painted umbrella?" asked Hannah's father. "The umbrella was orange with green stripes. It would have spoiled my blue-and-yellow color scheme. You said we couldn't afford a new one, so I painted it yellow. If I have time maybe I'll paint blue polka dots on it."

"That man!" said Hannah's mother. "Well, anyhow, the birdhouse and the fence stay white. When those judges see the blue-and-yellow-checkered restaurant and garage, that will be enough of a shock."

"What shock?" asked Hannah's father. "They'll

love it. What is there not to like?"

"I think everything looks swell," said Aunt Becky. "If I would be a judge, I would give you a prize right now."

The twelve-o'clock whistle blew. Hannah's mother went back inside. Skippy barked loudly from the cellar.

"Oh, I *wish* Skippy had a doghouse!" Hannah said to her father. "Then when he jumps up on people, he could go to his doghouse instead of the cellar, and he could still be outside."

"Look, Hannah!" Aunt Becky called from the porch. She had picked up her knitting needles again. Something big and red was hanging from them. "I am knitting you a guess-what!"

"Oh!" said Hannah. She couldn't think of anything else to say, so she said, "I have to go call Aggie!"

She ran over to the restaurant and into the kitchen.

"Aunt Becky's knitting me a guess-what," she whispered to her mother. "It's big and red."

"Look at *my* guess-what," said her mother. She

pointed to the windowsill. Her geranium plant had a knitted green jacket on the pot. It was a little too large and had fallen halfway down. Hannah's mother pulled it up. It fell back down again. "I also got a knitted bookmark," she said. "And wait till your father sees *his* guess-what!"

"But I don't like Aunt Becky's knitting so much," Hannah whispered. "It's always lumpy and bumpy and itchy if it's something to wear. And *my* guess-whats are *always* to wear. Yours aren't—you're lucky."

"Listen, Hannah," whispered her mother. "You know what I always tell you about Aunt Becky's knitting."

"I know," Hannah whispered back. "'Aunt Becky's knitting needles are filled with love.'" She went over to the kitchen sink and took a big bar of Ivory soap and washed her hands carefully so they wouldn't smell like paint or turpentine. She thought about calling Aggie again, but just then she heard footsteps in the restaurant.

"Lunch customers!" she said to her mother, peeking into the restaurant. "Can I take their orders?" She got a little pad and pencil and went over to a table by the window where a man and lady were sitting. They were reading the special on the blackboard out loud.

"I'll call Aggie after I wait on them," Hannah told herself. She ran over to the blackboard and drew the carrots and peas she hadn't had time to draw before *Let's Pretend*.

"Looks good," said the man.

"Smells good too," said the lady, and they both ordered week-end specials.

"Two week-end specials," Hannah wrote down on her little pad. She went back into the kitchen and read her mother the order. She ran into her bedroom and got her box of colored chalk. Then she ran back to the restaurant. Very carefully, she colored in her pictures on the blackboard.

"In color, it looks even more appetizing," said the lady.

Hannah's father was inside the restaurant now, showing the customers the certificate the restaurant had won last year. He had been very proud when he won it, just as he was proud of having been elected president of the Independent Benevolent Gas Dealers' Association of Rockland County a few months ago by the other gas-station owners. Hannah knew her father loved winning prizes and being elected to things. He had made a wooden frame in his workshop in the cellar and hung the certificate on the wall in the restaurant next to Hannah's mother's cross-stitched sampler.

The sampler said, LET ME LIVE IN THE HOUSE BY THE SIDE OF THE ROAD AND BE A FRIEND TO MAN.

The certificate said, CLEANEST PLACE ON ROUTE 9W.

"Looks like we picked a good place to stop," said the lady. "Friendly and clean. That's a good combination!"

"Actually anybody can win Cleanest Place," said Hannah's father. "That's easy—all you have to do is keep the place clean. But what I really want to win even more is Most Attractive Place on Route 9W. For Most Attractive you have to use your brain. You have to think of a way to make your place stand out."

"Oh, those blue and yellow shingles stand out, all right!" said the man.

"They match the gas pumps," said Hannah's father proudly. "That's where I got my idea for my color scheme. Wait till the judges see it—they'll faint!"

Just then another car pulled up in front of the restaurant. This time four people came in.

Hannah's father went into the kitchen to help Hannah's mother, and Hannah took the new orders.

"Four more roast-beef specials!" she said, running into the kitchen with her pad.

She ran back and forth from the restaurant to the kitchen as she set the tables, brought out silver ware, paper napkins, baskets of bread, and pats of butter. Her mother and father were busy slicing the roast beef, mashing the potatoes, and putting the hot steaming gravy over the meat and potatoes.

After the customers had finished, Hannah helped clear the tables and served slices of pie à la mode and mugs of hot coffee. She carried the mugs one at a time too.

Then Hannah watched her mother add up the bills and ring up the money in the cash register.

She loved to hear the bell jingle and to watch the drawer pop open. Hannah always thought you could never run out of money as long as you had a cash register.

She brought the customers their change and waved as they went out the door.

"I don't know what was better, the food or the waitress," one man said as he left. Hannah smiled and went over to clear the tables. She found a shiny quarter on each one.

"Hey—I got two quarters for tips!" Hannah yelled to her mother. "Fifty cents!"

"You earned it," said her mother. "You worked hard."

Hannah put the quarters in her pocket and started to clear the tables off. The phone rang and her mother answered it.

"It's for you," said her mother. "It's Aggie."

Hannah ran over to the phone. "Aggie!" she yelled. "I was going to call you to find out which show you're going to, but first I had to paint two shingles on the garage and then I waited on a bunch of customers. I got two quarters for tips!"

"Oh, you're lucky, Hannah!" said Aggie. "I wish I lived at The Grand View Restaurant! But guess what! I saw Otto outside in the street and he says he'll come to the four-o'clock show with us and *he'll* take Skippy out on the stage."

"*Otto?*" said Hannah. "Take *my* dog? I don't even *like* Otto!"

"Me either," said Aggie. "But ever since you moved from our street to Grand View, sometimes I go to the show with Otto just to have somebody to walk with. Otto says he never gets embarrassed. And you and I could sit together in the audience and clap for Skippy."

Hannah thought a minute. She liked the idea of being able to clap for Skippy and sitting with her friend.

"My father says he'll bring us up to the restaurant for an ice-cream cone before the show," said Aggie. "And we could help you give Skippy his bath."

"Oh, Aggie—*good!* Okay—I *decided!* I'll go to the movies and take Skippy to the dog show both. I have to go tell Skippy now. See you later, Aggie!" Hannah hung up.

"I *decided*!" Hannah told her mother. "I'm going to the four-o'clock show! I'm taking Skippy to the dog show! Aggie and Otto are coming to help me give Skippy his bath and get an ice-cream cone!"

Hannah ran into the bathroom. She opened the trapdoor and ran down the inside stairs.

"Skippy, I *decided*!" she said when she got to the bottom. Skippy opened one eye. "I'm going to the four-o'clock show! You're going to be in the *dog show*! Aggie and Otto are going too!" Skippy opened his other eye. Hannah didn't mention the bath. She reached into her pocket.

"Look!" Hannah said. She held up the two quarters. "Fifty cents!" she said. "Those are the best tips I ever got!"

Skippy thumped his tail. He licked Hannah's face. He went back to sleep.

"Except for you, of course, Skippy," Hannah whispered, patting his head. "The customers who left you here when you were a little puppy left the very best tip of all."

Madame Butterfly

"It must be getting near two o'clock," Hannah's father said.

Two o'clock on a Saturday afternoon in Hannah's house meant only one thing: the opera.

"Time to relax a little and listen to music," said Hannah's father. "I never missed one yet."

He reached over to his box of White Owl Cigars.

"Hey—what's this purple thing?" he asked. "Who covered up my cigar box?"

"Guess what?" said Aunt Becky. "It's a jacket!"

"A *jacket*? For a *cigar box*?"

"For the president of the Independent Benevolent Gas Dealers' Association of Rockland County's cigar box!"

Hannah's father stared at the purple cover. Then he slipped it off and took out a White Owl Cigar. Aunt Becky put the jacket back on.

"I knitted it *last* week while listening to the opera," she said. "I listen every Saturday too. I sing along."

"I already listened to *Let's Pretend*," said Hannah. "I think I'll go outside and watch for Aggie."

"You really should listen to the opera, Hannah," said Aunt Becky. "Opera is very cultural. Operas have stories too. You like stories. I'll tell you the story. Come, listen, Hannah darling."

Hannah remembered that Aunt Becky was company. So she sat down in the living room with her father and Aunt Becky. Then she jumped up.

"I have to go see if my mother needs me first," said Hannah. She ran into the restaurant where her mother was setting out new bottles of ketchup and jars of mustard.

"Need any help?" she asked. "I saw Daddy's guess-what," she said in a lower voice. "I don't think he likes it so much. He'll have to take it off and put it back on every time he wants to smoke a cigar."

"Good," said her mother. "Then maybe he'll smoke less stinkers." Hannah laughed. She always thought it was funny when her mother called her father's cigars "stinkers."

"You helped plenty already today," said Hannah's mother. "Go keep Aunt Becky company. She's a real opera lover like your father. The three of you can listen together."

"I don't like to listen to the opera," Hannah whispered into her mother's ear. "Daddy always makes it too loud."

"Just ask him to make it lower," said Hannah's mother. "The way I do."

"But he always says, 'That's the beauty of it,'" said Hannah. "You know."

"Just turn it down a little yourself, then," said Hannah's mother.

"Daddy will turn it back up," said Hannah. "That's why I usually like to go to the two-o'clock show."

"But today you're going to the four-o'clock

show," said her mother. "At least listen till Aggie comes—then you can excuse yourself and give Skippy his bath."

"Yoo-hoo," Aunt Becky called from the living room. "Time to come in and listen to the opera, Hannah darling."

"Okay," said Hannah to her mother. "I'll listen. But if Daddy makes it too loud and I can't stand it, I'm coming back out."

Hannah went into the living room with her father and Aunt Becky.

Her father turned the radio on. He went over and sat in his favorite chair next to his fish tank. He turned the fish-tank lights on.

"You see this, Becky?" he asked. "This is my two-way aquarium. I cut a hole in the wall and fitted it in this way especially. We can sit in the living room and see it from one side. The customers can sit at the tables in the restaurant and see it from the other side. Everybody can enjoy it. That's the beauty of it."

"Oh, it *is* beautiful," said Aunt Becky. "That's some swell fish tank!"

"If you think it's beautiful now, wait till you see it later," said Hannah's father. "Now that Hannah finished the last two shingles, all I have to do before the judges come is clean my aquarium."

"Don't forget to let me take the goldfish out with the little fishnet," said Hannah.

"*Hello, everybody!*" boomed a voice from the radio. "This is Milton Cross bringing you the Metropolitan Opera of the Air."

"Ah!" said Hannah's father. He leaned back in his chair.

"Oh, the opera!" said Aunt Becky. "How I *love* the opera!" She sat in another chair with her knitting needles and her red wool in her lap.

"I think I'll go get a drink of water," said Hannah. Her father had made the radio very loud. Milton Cross sounded like he was yelling.

From the kitchen, Hannah yelled back, "It's too loud!"

She walked out of the kitchen and was just going into the restaurant when she heard Aunt Becky call.

"Hannah, Hannah darling," called Aunt Becky. "Come quick."

Hannah ran back into the living room. She thought something had happened.

"Don't leave," said Aunt Becky. "It's *Madame Butterfly*! My favorite opera!"

"Mine too," said Hannah's father.

"You shouldn't miss it," said Aunt Becky. "*Madame Butterfly* is a beautiful story. Stay. Listen. I'll tell you all about it."

"Milton Cross is telling the story *now*," said Hannah's father. He was trying to listen.

"But I tell it better," said Aunt Becky. "I know *Madame Butterfly* backward and forward. Word for word. I can sing it better than all of them. It's a love story," she said to Hannah. "But such a sad one."

Hannah didn't like sad love stories. She was sorry she had come back into the living room. Now she didn't know how to leave politely. So she stayed. She sat on the edge of her chair and tried to think of another good excuse for leaving. She wished Aggie would hurry up and come.

"And now," said Milton Cross, "the golden curtain goes up on Act One of *Madame Butterfly*."

"Ooh!" said Hannah. "A golden curtain!"

"Ah!" said Hannah's father. "It's beginning!" He took the paper ring off his cigar and handed it to Hannah. Hannah put it on her finger.

Aunt Becky picked up her knitting needles and her wool. She turned to Hannah.

"I know the whole opera by heart," she said. "If the soprano ever got sick on the last minute, they could call on me to take over."

Aunt Becky's knitting needles clicked together loudly. Hannah thought they sounded like the castanets in the rhythm band in school.

The opera stars began to sing. Aunt Becky sang along with them. When Aunt Becky hit a high note, Hannah felt like holding her ears.

Hannah's father had been smoking his cigar and listening with his eyes shut. Now he opened his eyes. He groaned a little.

"What's the matter?" asked Aunt Becky. "Got indigestion from eating so many matzo balls this morning?"

Hannah and her father looked at each other and quickly looked away from each other so they wouldn't laugh.

Madame Butterfly and Aunt Becky sang together some more. Aunt Becky hit another high note and Skippy barked. Aunt Becky stopped singing. She looked worried.

"Your big dog can't come up and jump on me again, can he?" she asked.

"Don't worry, Aunt Becky," said Hannah. "He's in the cellar and the door's closed."

Madame Butterfly and Aunt Becky sang together some more. Aunt Becky hit another high note. Then suddenly Hannah looked up and saw Aggie Branagan and Otto Zimmer standing in the doorway between the kitchen and the living room. Their mouths were open and they were staring.

"Aggie!" said Hannah. "I didn't even hear you come in!" She jumped up and ran into the kitchen and out to the restaurant with them.

Mr. Branagan was in the restaurant talking to Hannah's mother. He was telling her how much he liked the blue and yellow checkered shingles.

She was telling him how much she didn't.

"Ah, Mademoiselle Hannah!" said Mr. Branagan. "I haven't seen you in a long time. We really miss you in the old neighborhood. Where's your dad?"

"He's listening to the opera in the living room with my Aunt Becky," said Hannah.

Madame Butterfly hit a high note and Aunt Becky joined her again. Hannah could feel her face get red. Skippy barked again.

"Aunt Becky has a terrible voice," Hannah whispered to her mother.

"Shh," said Hannah's mother. "Becky always wanted to be an opera singer when she was young. Don't say anything that would hurt her feelings."

"I won't," said Hannah. "I was just telling *you*."

"Your Aunt Becky," said Mr. Branagan. "I don't believe I've had the pleasure. I never met a lady who aspired to sing opera before. Perhaps she would care to join me in a bottle of beer." He walked into the kitchen.

"Get yourselves some ice cream, kids," he called over his shoulder. "We've got plenty of time."

He went into the living room. "Hey, Izzie, are you busy?" Hannah could hear him call to her father.

"Would you like some ice cream now?" asked Hannah's mother. "Or would you like to give Skippy his bath first?"

"Let's go down and see him," said Hannah. "He must be lonesome down there. I wish we didn't have to give him a bath, though. He really hates baths."

"That's why his coat doesn't shine," said Hannah's mother. "He hasn't had a bath since the last time he jumped out of the basin and ran away with all those soapsuds on him and never got rinsed off. If you take a dog to a dog show, his coat should shine."

Hannah explained to Aggie and Otto. "Whenever we try to give him a bath, he always jumps up out of the water and runs up the mountain and hides. And when he comes home, all leaves and things are stuck to him. That's why I always hate even *trying* to give him a bath."

"In the cellar it will be better," said Hannah's

mother. "We'll bring the basin of water down. If we keep the door closed, there's no place he can run to. And I won't have to worry about him getting the floor all wet in the restaurant."

"And don't forget we're going to *help* you," said Aggie.

"And I'll hold him so he doesn't jump out," said Otto. "I'm stronger than you girls. That's why I always get to hold the flag in assembly."

"Otto thinks he's a big shot," Aggie whispered in Hannah's ear.

"You three go down the outside steps," said Hannah's mother, "so you won't disturb the opera lovers. I'll follow with the basin of water after you're in."

Hannah, Aggie, and Otto ran outside and went down the outside steps. They could hear Madame Butterfly and Aunt Becky all the way down.

When they got into the cellar, Skippy jumped up and licked Hannah's face. His tail was wagging and his eyes were shining. Hannah patted his head. Aggie and Otto patted Skippy too, and he licked their hands.

"He likes me!" said Aggie.

"He *loves* me!" said Otto.

"Isn't he friendly?" asked Hannah. "Aunt Becky got scared of him when he jumped on her, just like all the grown-ups do. They don't know he's just trying to make friends—that's why he has to stay down here so much. My mother was right about his coat, though—it *is* terrible."

"Let's go back up and help bring the stuff down," said Otto. "Then we can get our ice cream too."

"We'll be right back, Skippy," said Hannah. They ran out, closed the door carefully, and ran back up the steps and around to the front door of the restaurant.

Hannah opened the ice-cream box.

"Vanilla," said Aggie.

"Chocolate," said Otto.

Hannah got out one MelOrol of each flavor. She unrolled the paper wrappings and put the MelOrols into cones. She handed the cones to Aggie and Otto and closed the ice-cream box.

Suddenly the music from the living room got

very loud. Then it got lower. Then it got louder.

Hannah, Aggie, and Otto ran through the kitchen into the living room to see what was happening. Hannah's mother was turning the knob on the radio.

"It's too *loud*," she said.

"But that's the beauty of it," said Hannah's father. He got up and turned the radio back up.

"Besides," he whispered to Hannah's mother as he passed her, "how can I hear with Becky singing so loud?"

Aunt Becky and Madame Butterfly were singing a duet.

Mr. Branagan was listening and drinking a bottle of beer.

"Where's *your* ice cream, Mademoiselle Hannah?" he asked. "It's my treat."

"Thanks, Mr. Branagan," said Hannah, "but I don't like MelOrols. I just like ice cream from Eagle's Ice Cream Parlor."

"Then if it's ever my good fortune to meet you on Main Street," said Mr. Branagan, "we'll sashay into Eagle's and get you a double dip. And how about you, Aunt Becky?" he asked. "Ice cream should be soothing to the throat of a singer such as yourself."

Aunt Becky smiled and said a vanilla would suit her just fine. Hannah's mother went to get it.

Hannah asked her father to blow smoke rings while she waited for Aggie and Otto to finish their cones. She watched her father's smoke rings float up to the ceiling like clouds. She tried to catch them.

Hannah's mother came back with Aunt Becky's MelOrol.

"Pyoo!" she said. "That cigar is a real stinker."

Hannah and Aggie giggled.

Aunt Becky started her cone just as Aggie and Otto finished theirs.

"Time to get Skippy ready for the dog show, Ma," said Hannah.

"Did you say dog show, Hannah?" asked Aunt Becky. "What dog show?"

"There's a dog show at the four-o'clock movies," said Hannah.

"Oh, I love dog shows," said Aunt Becky. "In Brooklyn, my little Poopala-darling wins every dog show I take her to. She behaves like a lady and she never jumps up on anybody. I hope your dog should do the same." Aunt Becky took another lick of her ice-cream cone and sang another duet with Madame Butterfly.

"Maybe you would like to go to the dog show too?" Hannah's father asked Becky. Hannah's mother looked at him and frowned. "Then I could hear the rest of the opera in peace," he grumbled under his breath.

"Shh!" whispered Hannah's mother. "Is that a nice way to talk?"

"Is this a nice way to listen to an opera?" Hannah's father whispered back. "What a racket!" He took a big puff on his cigar.

"Pyoo!" said Hannah's mother again, holding her nose. "What a stinker!" She walked into the kitchen. Hannah, Aggie, and Otto followed her.

"Hannah!" called Aunt Becky. "Wait a minute!"

Hannah went to the doorway between the kitchen and the living room.

"Good luck with your dog," said Aunt Becky. "And don't worry about missing the rest of the opera. Tonight I'll sing you every note you missed!"

The Chase

"Time to get started with Skippy's bath now," said Hannah's mother. She filled a kettle with warm water. She gave Hannah a basin. She gave Aggie a bar of Ivory soap. She gave Otto an old towel.

"Come," she said.

Hannah, Aggie, and Otto followed Hannah's mother out the door and down the outside stairs to the cellar. They all went in and closed the door.

As soon as Skippy saw the basin and the kettle, he ran and hid under Hannah's father's worktable.

"See how smart he is?" asked Hannah. "He knows he's going to get a bath now. And he doesn't like to take a bath. See, I told you. Come on, Skippy. Come on out." Hannah bent down and put her hands out toward Skippy. "We won't hurt you, I promise. It's just to make your coat shine so you can win the dog show."

Hannah's mother put the basin on the table. She poured the water into the basin. She dropped the cake of soap into the water. "So it'll melt a little and be easier to suds him," she explained.

"Okay, Skippy," said Hannah's mother. "In you go."

Skippy was still hiding under the table.

"You'll have to go in under the table and get him," said Hannah's mother.

Hannah bent down and went in under the table. "Come on, Skippy," she begged. "Come on out. We won't hurt you—I promise."

Skippy came out slowly.

Hannah's mother picked him up. "You'll all have to help me hold him," she said.

Skippy made funny noises in the water.

"Ooh, he doesn't like it," said Aggie.

"Give him a shampoo, Hannah," said Hannah's mother.

Hannah picked up the bar of soap and rubbed

it all over Skippy. She rubbed gently. Skippy looked at Hannah. His tail didn't wag. His eyes didn't shine.

"I'm sorry, Skippy," said Hannah. "I know you don't like it. But it's not so bad. I won't let any soap get in your eyes, don't worry. It's just to make you look better, Skippy."

"He'll feel better too when he's clean," said Hannah's mother.

"Ooh—I have to go to the bathroom, Hannah," said Aggie. "I'll be right back."

Hannah didn't hear Aggie because she was so busy trying to cover Skippy with soapsuds without scaring him.

But Hannah's mother heard Aggie.

"Use the inside steps, Aggie," said Hannah's mother. "Push the trapdoor up and you'll be right in the bathroom."

But Aggie had already started to open the cellar door to the outside steps. Before she could close it, Skippy jumped up out of the basin.

"Hold on, Otto!" cried Hannah.

But Skippy slid out of everyone's hands. He ran

through the open door just as Aggie was trying to close it.

"Oh, *Aggie—Otto!*" said Hannah. "He got away!"

"Catch him!" said Hannah's mother. "He's covered with soapsuds—just like last time! We have to rinse him off!"

Hannah, Aggie, and Otto chased Skippy up the outside steps, but Skippy was too fast for them.

He ran across Route 9W and headed for the mountain road.

"Look both ways before crossing!" called Hannah's mother.

Hannah looked both ways, and then Hannah, Aggie, and Otto began to run after Skippy.

Skippy turned up at the mountain road.

Big white fluffs of soapsuds were falling off him as he ran. Soap bubbles floated up into the air.

Hannah, Aggie, and Otto ran around the soapsuds and through the bubbles.

"I'm sorry I didn't use the inside steps, Hannah," Aggie called as she ran. "I haven't been up here in such a long time, I forgot about them."

"I'm sorry I didn't hold on better," called Otto.

"The soapsuds were so slippery, he just slid right out of my hands!"

"You couldn't help it," Hannah called back to Aggie and Otto. "It always happens to me too."

Hannah, Aggie, and Otto were panting and puffing, but they kept running. Soon they were near the top of the mountain. Skippy was still ahead. Hannah saw a rainbow on one great big soap bubble shimmering in the sunshine, but she couldn't stop to catch it.

They came to the very top of the mountain.

Skippy ran through the high grass into Hannah's secret place.

"Stop!" said Hannah to Aggie and Otto. "That's my secret place! Nobody can go in there but me. Skippy!" she called. "Skippy, *come out!*"

In a minute, Skippy came back out, but Skippy didn't look like Skippy anymore. Grass, leaves, and pine needles were stuck to him.

"Skippy!" said Hannah. "Oh, Skippy! Look at you! You look terrible!"

Skippy came over and licked Hannah's face. His tail was wagging again. His eyes were shining.

"Oh, Skippy!" said Hannah, picking off a pine needle. "Now you'll never win the dog show. You're a mess!"

"We better catch him and take him back and rinse him off," said Otto.

As soon as Otto said "catch him," Skippy began to run again.

"Skippy, stop!" said Hannah. "Wait! Wait for us, Skippy!"

This time Skippy was running *down* the mountain.

Hannah, Aggie, and Otto ran after him. The faster they ran, the faster Skippy ran

"We'll never catch him," said Aggie.

When they got near the bottom of the mountain road, Hannah called, "Look both ways before crossing, Skippy!"

They all crossed Route 9W again, but this time Skippy didn't run toward The Grand View Restaurant. He kept running down, toward the river road.

"Skippy!" called Hannah. "Come back! Where are you going now? You've never been down the river road yet. My mother doesn't let me take you down there 'cause you can't swim." But Skippy kept on running.

Hannah, Aggie, and Otto kept running after him. Soon they were down by the river.

"Skippy!" called Hannah. "You ran all the way from the top of the mountain down to the river— and you're not supposed to! *Please* come home now and let us rinse you off. We'll never get to the dog show in time!"

Skippy raced across the sandy beach toward the edge of the water. Hannah, Aggie, and Otto were right behind him.

"Stop!" yelled Hannah.

Aggie stopped.

Otto stopped.

Hannah stopped.

Skippy kept on running.

"That's the *river*, Skippy!" yelled Hannah. "It's *water*! You don't even *like* water!"

Skippy disappeared.

For a minute, all they could see was his head. Then he turned around and looked back at them.

Hannah couldn't speak. She couldn't move.

"Look at Skippy's *eyes*!" said Aggie.

"Does he look surprised!" said Otto.

"Oh, Skippy!" wailed Hannah. "Don't drown!"

Then, all of a sudden, Skippy's front paws came up out of the water.

He began to paddle.

"He's giving himself a swimming lesson!" said Aggie.

"He can swim!" said Otto. "He taught himself!"

"Skippy!" called Hannah. "Swim back!"

Skippy swam back to shore. He ran out of the water. He ran over to Hannah. He was dripping all over. But his tail was wagging. And his eyes were shining. He jumped up and licked Hannah's face. He shook himself. Water sprayed all over Hannah and Aggie and Otto.

"Skippy!" said Hannah. "You rinsed yourself off!"

"Run!" said Otto. "Run home!"

Hannah, Aggie, and Otto began to run. They ran away from the river, across the sand, and toward the river road.

"Keep running!" said Otto "He'll follow *us* now! Catch us, Skippy, catch us!"

Hannah, Aggie, and Otto kept running.

Skippy ran after them.

They ran toward The Grand View Restaurant.

Hannah kept looking over her shoulder to make sure Skippy was behind them. But she kept running too.

They ran into the restaurant. Skippy ran in behind them.

"Oh, he's getting the whole floor wet!" said Hannah's mother. She ran and got another towel.

"Ma! Skippy had a swimming lesson!" said Hannah. "And *he was his own teacher!*"

The Dog Show

"Skippy looks beautiful now!" said Hannah. They had dried him and brushed his coat.

"He feels nice and smooth," said Otto, patting Skippy's back.

"He shines!" said Aggie.

"It was the bath and all the exercise," said Hannah's mother. "Running is good exercise. But now you have to hurry. Mr. Branagan is waiting to drive you to the movies and I'll pick you up when it's over."

"But what about Skippy?" asked Hannah. "How'll I get him home after the dog show without missing Shirley Temple?"

"I called up the movies while you were gone," said Hannah's mother. "They told me to allow half an hour for the dog show, so I'll be waiting outside with the car at four-thirty. All you have to do is bring Skippy out to the car and I'll take him back home. Then you can go back in and see the movie." Hannah's mother bent down and attached a leash to Skippy's collar.

"Oh, Skippy hates leashes!" said Hannah.

"For a dog show, you have to have one," said Hannah's mother. "Besides, with this dog, you can't take any more chances." She handed the leash to Hannah. Hannah bent down.

"It's just for the dog show, Skippy," she whispered. "You can take it off as soon as you get home."

Hannah heard a horn.

"All aboard!" called Mr. Branagan from outside the restaurant.

Hannah, Skippy, Aggie, and Otto all ran out and got inside the car with Mr. Branagan. Skippy sat next to Hannah and thumped his tail on the floor.

"Skippy loves to go for rides," Hannah told Aggie.

Hannah's father came out and looked in the window of the car.

"Good luck," he said.

"Thanks," said Hannah. "Don't let the judges come while I'm gone!"

"If they do," said her father, "I'll make them stay till you get back!"

Mr. Branagan revved up the engine.

"And good luck to you too, Izzie," he said. "Whenever the judges come. Your checkerboard idea is a real knockout!"

Hannah's father smiled. "Everybody likes it but Mollie," he said. "She says it makes her dizzy." He stopped talking a minute as he heard two loud voices sing out.

"Act Three must be starting!" he said and ran back inside.

Mr. Branagan revved the engine again.

"Wait a minute!" Hannah heard her mother's voice call. Her mother came running out to the car and handed in three Hershey bars to Hannah, Aggie, and Otto.

"To eat while you watch the movie," she said.

"Ooh, thanks!" said Aggie. "With *almonds*—my favorite kind!"

"Mine too," said Hannah. "I never eat chocolate bars without them."

"It's fun to come here!" said Otto.

Hannah's mother stuck her head in the window.

"And you behave yourself!" she said, pointing at Skippy. "Watch your manners—and don't jump on anybody!" Skippy thumped his tail on the floor inside the car again, and Mr. Branagan drove off.

They drove down 9W from Grand View to South Nyack. Mr. Branagan turned right on Cornelison Avenue, then left on Broadway. Hannah loved Broadway because the branches of the tall trees on one side arched over and touched the branches of the tall trees on the other side. She always told herself the trees were holding hands. She sat back and looked out of the back window.

"Look, Skippy, isn't it pretty?" she whispered.

"We're driving under a tree tunnel—with green lace on all the branches, and you can see the sun through the holes in the lace!"

Skippy licked Hannah's nose.

"I hope you remember to have good manners," Hannah whispered into Skippy's ear. "Aunt Becky's dog Poopala-darling does, and she wins every dog show in Brooklyn."

"Oh, Hannah, I can't wait!" said Aggie. "A dog show and Shirley Temple all in the same day! I'm so glad you're going to sit in the audience with me."

"I am too," said Hannah. "I'm glad I don't have to go up on the stage with Skippy, though. I really get embarrassed going up on a stage—in school in assembly I didn't like it at all."

"Me too," said Aggie. "I get shy."

"You girls are scaredy-cats," said Otto. "I'm not scared. I'm *glad* I'm going to take Skippy up on the stage. I *never* get embarrassed."

"You think you're a big shot, Otto," said Aggie.

"I *am*," said Otto.

"Okay, kids," said Mr. Branagan. "We're here!" He stopped in front of the movie.

"We're here, Skippy!" said Hannah. "You're going to be in a dog show! Oh, I hope you win!"

Aggie, Otto, Hannah, and Skippy all got out of the car.

"So long, folks!" said Mr. Branagan. "And good luck, Mademoiselle Hannah and Monsieur Skippy!" He waved out the window of the car as he drove off.

"Sometimes your father talks just like a movie star!" Hannah told Aggie. She waved back to Mr. Branagan.

Hannah, Aggie, and Otto ran to the ticket window and each paid a dime for a ticket.

"Take your dog around to the side door," said the lady in the ticket booth. "That's where the kids showing dogs are lined up. You'd better hurry. Everyone's there already."

Hannah, Aggie, Otto, and Skippy ran around to the side. There was a long line of kids and dogs. Most of the dogs were barking. Skippy didn't bark. He just wagged his tail.

A girl in front of Skippy had a little white poodle with curly hair. The girl had curls like Shirley Temple, and she and the dog wore matching pink satin ribbons.

"My dog's a thoroughbred," the girl said to Hannah. "Is your dog a thoroughbred?"

"I don't know what a thoroughbred *is*," said Hannah.

"My dog has papers," said the girl. "Has your dog got papers?"

"What are dog papers?" asked Hannah.

"They tell that the dog is a thoroughbred," said the girl. "If it isn't a thoroughbred, it's a *mutt*. My mother said I shouldn't let any mutts get near my dog because she's so teeny and delicate. Keep away from that big dog, Coco."

Coco growled at Skippy. Skippy wagged his tail.

"Oh, Skippy wouldn't hurt anybody," said Hannah. "He's *friendly*. I don't think he's got any papers, though."

"Then he's a *mutt*," said the girl. "Mutts are dumb."

"Skippy's not dumb," said Hannah. "He's smart."

"What can he do?" asked the girl.

Hannah tried to think of something Skippy could do.

"*My* dog can beg, fetch, sit, lie, roll over, and jump through a hoop," said the girl. "And she's very well-mannered."

Hannah thought of something. "Skippy can swim," she said. "He just taught himself this morning."

"We *saw* him," said Aggie.

"He swam in the *river*," said Otto.

"Well, he can't swim up on the stage," said the girl. "*My* father's the mayor of the town."

Coco growled at Hannah, Aggie, and Otto. She growled some more at Skippy.

Hannah looked at the mayor's daughter.

"*My* father's the president of the Independent Benevolent Gas Dealers' Association of Rockland County," she said.

Hannah handed Skippy's leash to Otto. "Well, good-bye," she said. She bent down and patted Skippy's head.

"Don't worry, Skippy," she whispered. "I like mutts the best. I don't like that Coco at all—she's *unfriendly*. I have to go inside now with Aggie, but that's just so I can clap for you. Now, remember: Don't jump on anybody. Behave like a good dog and have manners!" Skippy licked Hannah's chin.

Hannah stood up. She and Aggie ran around to the front of the movies.

"Save me a seat!" Otto called after them.

"Ooh, I can't stand that girl!" said Aggie. "She's so stuck-up, with her curls and pink ribbons."

Aggie and Hannah both had straight hair.

"Her *dog* is even stuck-up," said Hannah. They ran into the lobby.

"I even like *Otto* better than that girl," said Aggie. "That's how much I can't stand her." They gave their tickets to the ticket taker. He tore them in half and told Hannah and Aggie to save their stubs.

When they went into the theater, almost all the empty seats were taken. The only row Hannah and Aggie found with three empty seats together was the last row over on the right side.

"I hope we can see from here," said Hannah. "I never sat so far back."

"Me either," said Aggie. "I never sat way over at the end of the row like this either."

They sat down and saved a seat for Otto.

The manager of the movies was standing in the middle of the stage.

"Quiet, boys and girls," he was saying. "If you will only be quiet, we can start. *Quiet*, I said!" He clapped his hands together loudly.

"He sounds like Miss Hinckle in school before assembly," whispered Aggie.

"These kids are behaving worse than in assembly," said Hannah.

"I guess they're all excited over the dog show," said Aggie. "I'm excited too!"

"NOW!" said the manager. "The dog show will begin! Clap loudest for your favorite dog, because the one that gets the most applause will be the winner. The winner gets the blue ribbon."

"I'm just going to clap for Skippy," said Aggie. "Because he's your dog and you're my friend."

Hannah thought about what Aggie had said. Secretly, she wanted to clap just for Skippy too. But whenever Hannah watched a contest, she always ended up clapping for everybody so she wouldn't feel like she was playing favorites. She always thought how she would feel if she was the one getting clapped for and nobody clapped for her. Besides, if everybody clapped just for their own dog, then Hannah and Aggie would be the only ones to clap for Skippy. And then Skippy wouldn't win. So Hannah thought if she clapped for all the other people's dogs and they all clapped for Skippy, then maybe Skippy would have a chance to win.

All kinds of dogs came out with all kinds of kids. There were big dogs and little dogs with big kids and little kids. Some of the kids looked a little shy or embarrassed, the way Hannah and Aggie felt they would feel on a stage, but most of them looked proud. Some had fancy dogs and some had plain dogs. Some had dogs that did tricks. Hannah clapped for all of them. She clapped for so many dogs, her hands began to get tired.

"But I'll save my loudest and best clapping for when Skippy comes out," she said to herself. "I'll just play favorites a little."

"Where are Otto and Skippy?" Aggie whispered to Hannah. "It's taking such a long time!"

"I don't know," said Hannah. "But remember— we were almost late. We were the last ones."

The mayor's daughter came out with Coco. They got a lot of applause.

"Boo," said Aggie into Hannah's ear.

Hannah couldn't decide what to do. She remembered her promise to clap for everybody. So she clapped one clap, very low.

"Skippy and Otto should be next," said Aggie.

Hannah heard a muffled sound behind the curtain. She got ready to clap her very best clapping in case it was Skippy. Suddenly Skippy came running out—alone. His leash was trailing behind him. He ran across the stage toward the manager. Otto came running out after him.

"Catch him!" said the manager. "Dogs aren't allowed to run loose in this dog show!" Skippy ran over to the manager and jumped up on him.

"Oof!" said the manager. "Down!" Otto tried to grab Skippy's leash, but Skippy turned around and ran in the opposite direction. Otto turned and ran after him. The manager ran behind Otto.

At first the kids in the audience were so surprised, they all got quiet. Hannah's heart started to pound so hard she thought everyone would hear it.

At the end of the stage, Skippy ran down the steps and into the audience. The kids all started to yell as Skippy ran up the left aisle with Otto and the manager running after him.

Hannah didn't move. Skippy didn't stop moving. He ran to the end of the aisle on the left, then across the back to the center and down the center aisle. By now the ushers had joined Otto and the manager chasing after Skippy. The kids in the audience were screaming and laughing. Skippy got to the front row and turned right. Some kids jumped up and started to chase Skippy too.

Hannah slid down in her seat. She was so embarrassed, she didn't even want to see what happened next. She closed her eyes.

Skippy was now racing up the right aisle with Otto and the manager and the ushers and some kids behind him. The kids in their seats were screaming so loud, Hannah held her ears. Suddenly she felt a big wet tongue on her cheek. She opened her eyes. It was Skippy! He was standing on his two back legs with his front legs up on Hannah's shoulders, and he was licking her face—in front of the whole audience!

"He found you, Hannah—he found you!" said Aggie.

The kids were screaming and laughing even louder than before. They were jumping up and down in their seats.

Hannah wished she was invisible.

The manager shook his finger at Hannah and Otto and Aggie.

"This dumb mutt is the worst behaved animal I have ever seen!" he said. *"Remove this animal from the premises at once!"*

Skippy began to run again.

Hannah jumped up. Aggie jumped up. Hannah, Aggie, and Otto chased Skippy out into the lobby and right out the front door of the movies.

"Just like before!" said Otto. "Up on the mountain!"

"And down by the river!" said Aggie.

"Skippy!" yelled Hannah. "I'm not going to chase you one more time today! You're really going to get it this time!"

"Skippy! In here!" called a voice. Hannah looked up and saw her mother parked by the curb. The door of the car was open. Skippy jumped into the car and began to lick Hannah's mother's face. Hannah slammed the door shut behind him.

"You wait till I get you home, Skippy!" said Hannah through the window. Skippy got down on the floor.

"What's the matter?" asked Hannah's mother. "How was the dog show?"

"Terrible!" said Hannah. "I clapped for everybody else's dog, and I didn't even get a chance to clap for *my* dog. He didn't get one clap—not from me, not from anybody. *He ran away again!* He jumped on the manager! The manager yelled at me! I was so embarrassed—and I wasn't even on the stage!"

"Ran away?" asked Hannah's mother. "Inside? With a leash?"

"I was holding on," said Otto, "but just when the manager said, 'It's your turn,' that bratty girl and her bratty dog came backstage, and she said 'Nyaa nyaa nyaa, we're gonna win!' I got mad and started to say 'Nyaa nyaa nyaa, no you're not!' and that's when Skippy pulled away from me— I don't even know how. And he ran out on the stage without me, and I couldn't catch hold of his leash again. Was I embarrassed!"

Hannah looked at Otto. Could Otto get embarrassed too? His eyes looked red-rimmed. Did Otto ever *cry*, Hannah wondered. She was so surprised, she forgot to be angry at Skippy for a minute.

"Well, Skippy *does* have a mind of his own," said Hannah's mother. "Maybe he just didn't want to be in a dog show. Now you three better hurry back in so you don't miss the picture. Mollie's taxi will be here again to pick you up when the movie is over."

"*Go back in?*" said Hannah. "I'm not going back in there. I'm *never* going back in there. Everybody was laughing. The manager yelled at me!"

"You paid your dime," said Hannah's mother. "So you're just as entitled to see the movie as anybody else who bought a ticket. If the manager says anything, you just tell him to call Nyack 714, and I'll tell him money doesn't grow on trees. The dog show is over. Forget it. Go back in and see the movie."

"We've still got our ticket stubs," said Otto.

"Come on, Hannah," said Aggie. "We never missed a Shirley Temple movie. Let's go back!"

Skippy stuck his head out the car window.

Hannah shook her finger at him.

"*You mutt, you!*" she yelled. "You behaved terri-
bly! I was ashamed of you! You ran away again!
And you jumped up again! And . . ." Hannah
looked into Skippy's eyes. She thought they
looked sad. ". . . and . . . Oh, Skippy, *I love you!*"
Hannah threw her arms around Skippy's neck.
She hugged him, hard.

Aggie and Otto ran over and patted Skippy's
head.

Skippy licked Hannah's face. He licked Aggie's
face. He licked Otto's face.

"Thanks, Otto," said Hannah. "You tried. I'm
glad you said, 'Nyaa nyaa nyaa' back to that girl.
Her dog probably *did* win."

"Boo," said Aggie. "I still like Skippy best."

"Thanks, Aggie," said Hannah.

Hannah's mother started the car.

"Enjoy the movie," she said. "I'll see you later."

As the car drove off down Broadway, Hannah,
Aggie, and Otto watched Skippy's head watching
them out the window. They waved till the car
was too far away to see him anymore.

Then they ran back inside the lobby and showed

their stubs to the ticket taker. They ran into the darkened theater and sat in the three end seats in the last row on the right. They pulled the wrappers off their Hershey bars.

"He has no manners and he always runs away and he doesn't behave right," thought Hannah. "But he's *not* a dumb mutt! Out of this whole big audience, he found me! That's really *smart!*" And she crunched her chocolate bar with almonds and pretended she was Shirley Temple tap-dancing across the screen.

Goldfish and More Butterfly

"Mollie's taxi!" Hannah heard when they came out of the movie. Hannah, Aggie, and Otto piled into the car.

"Where's Skippy?" asked Hannah. "Did the judges come yet?"

"Skippy's fast asleep in the cellar," said her mother. "He was exhausted. He's been sleeping ever since I brought him home. We even had a noisy bus while you were gone and he didn't wake up. And no, the judges didn't come yet."

"So how was the movie?" asked Hannah's mother after they had dropped Aggie and Otto off on their street in Nyack. Hannah waved to

Aggie and Otto out of the window of the car as long as she could see them.

"I loved it," said Hannah. "Shirley Temple was so cute! Grandma will love it too." Every Saturday Hannah wrote to her grandmother in New York City to tell her about the movie she had seen. Her grandmother said it was like going to the movies free.

"You can write and tell her about it now," said Hannah's mother, pulling up to The Grand View Restaurant.

"As soon as I see if Skippy's all right!" said Hannah. She ran around to the side of the restaurant, opened the gate in the latticework fence, and ran down the outside steps to the cellar door. She opened the door and tiptoed in. Skippy was lying curled up on the rag rug with his tail touching his nose again.

"You awake yet, Skippy?" Hannah whispered. Skippy's eyes were closed. The hairs on his tail blew up and down every time he exhaled.

"Boy!" whispered Hannah. "You really *are* tired!"

She tiptoed over to her father's worktable and looked for the pad and pencil she knew he always kept there. There were pieces of paper all over the worktable. They had drawings of buildings and lots of numbers.

"They all look like The Grand View Restaurant," thought Hannah. She felt around under them until she found the pad. Then she borrowed her father's pencil.

"Dear Skippy," she wrote. "I'm sorry I didn't clap and I yelled at you. I'll never make you be in a dog show again. After this we'll just run up and down the mountain and have fun together— okay? Love, Hannah." She thought a minute. Then she wrote, "P.S. Did you know you lost?" She thought another minute and erased the P.S. She left the note on the rug next to Skippy's nose and tiptoed up the inside staircase to write to her grandmother. At the top, she pushed on the trapdoor, but it didn't go up. Hannah started back down the stairs when suddenly the trapdoor opened. She looked up and saw her father.

"You can come up," said her father, "but shh . . ." He put a finger to his lips and nodded toward the bathtub.

Hannah ran back up the steps and into the bathroom. Her father put the trapdoor down while she ran over and looked into the tub. The bathtub was filled with goldfish.

"Oh, you're cleaning your aquarium without me!" said Hannah. "You always let me take the fish out of the aquarium with the little fishnet first when you do that!"

"But you weren't here when I took them out," said Hannah's father. "We had a bus, and after Mother, Becky, and I cleaned up all the stuff the bus people threw on the ground, Mother went to get you at the movies. Becky went to lie down to rest, and the only thing I had left to do for the judges was clean my aquarium. You know Mother doesn't like it when I put the fish in the tub . . ."

"Yes," said Hannah. "She always says, 'Goldfish in the bathtub again—Oh, that man!'"

"So I figured I'd just get them in and out fast before she even noticed it," her father continued.

"I got the aquarium all clean and sparkling, and I would have had the fish back in before you and Mother even got home, but ideas kept popping into my head for a project I'm working on, and I kept running up and down the cellar stairs to write down things I wanted to remember."

"Oh, I saw all the papers on your worktable!" said Hannah. "With a lot of numbers and pictures of buildings. They all looked like The Grand View Restaurant! What are they?"

Hannah's father looked startled. "You weren't supposed to see those," he said. "It's a new surprise I'm working on. I keep drawing it over till it comes out right."

"What is it?" asked Hannah. "Please tell."

"You know I never tell a surprise," said Hannah's father. "Because then the surprise wouldn't be a surprise."

"I know," said Hannah.

"Say, I didn't even get a chance to tell you how sorry I feel about the dog show," said her father. "Mother told me what happened. You must feel bad."

"I felt embarrassed when it happened," said Hannah. "At first I even got mad at Skippy. But I guess he just didn't feel like going on a stage—like me. So now I just feel bad because I clapped for everybody else's dog and I didn't get to clap for Skippy."

"Well, later, when Skippy wakes up, you and I will clap for him."

"Oh, good!" Hannah smiled at her father. "And I'm glad the judges didn't come while I was gone. I still hope you win your certificate for Most Attractive Place on Route 9W. The blue and yellow checks look so pretty."

"Thanks," said her father. "I don't know why Mother doesn't like it—what is there not to like?" He handed Hannah the little fishnet. "You can take the fish out of the bathtub now," he whispered. "Just put them into this pail of water and we'll take them over to the aquarium."

"Supper, everybody!" called Hannah's mother from the kitchen. "It's on the table!"

"Well, we'll do it right after we eat supper then," whispered Hannah's father. "But don't say anything to Mother about the fish before we eat—it might spoil her appetite." He opened the bathroom door and they went into the living room.

Just then Hannah's bedroom door opened and Aunt Becky came out.

"Whew!" she said. "I really got tired out from those noisy hooligans on the bus! Oh, Hannah darling—you poor child! It just broke my heart for you that your dog misbehaved at the dog show!"

"Oh, that's okay, Aunt Becky," said Hannah, but she could feel her face get hot. She was embarrassed to have Aunt Becky know about Skippy's bad manners.

"Hey—let's eat!" said Hannah's father.

"My father's the only grown-up who never worries about manners," thought Hannah. "I'm glad."

After supper, Hannah put all the leftover scraps on a paper plate and went down to the cellar to bring them to Skippy. But first she whispered in her father's ear, "Don't take the goldfish out till I come back up—okay?"

Skippy was still sleeping, so Hannah picked up his note and took it over to the worktable. She added a new P.S.: "I guess you're going to sleep all night, but here's a lot of scraps in case you wake up and get hungry."

When she went back upstairs, her father was not in the bathroom. Aunt Becky was knitting in the living room. The red guess-what was very long now and had lots of lumps and bumps.

Hannah's mother came into the living room and took a book out of the bookcase.

"Where's Daddy?" asked Hannah.

"A car came for gas," said her mother. "Why don't you practice your piano lessons now, so Aunt Becky can hear you?"

"I can't now," said Hannah. "I have to . . ." She stopped herself just in time.

"Oh, you take piano lessons!" said Aunt Becky. "That's very cultural."

"But I like playing rolls on the piano the best," said Hannah. She wished her father would hurry up. "I practice every day after school. On weekends, I like to play rolls."

Aunt Becky looked over her knitting. "What are piano rolls?" she asked.

Hannah went over to the old piano in one corner of the living room and opened the top of the piano bench. The inside was filled with Hannah's music books and with long rolls of white paper. She looked at Aunt Becky's long red guess-what again. Then she chose one of the paper rolls and took it out of the piano bench.

"This is a roll of music," she said. "I'll play it for you till my father comes back in."

She opened two little sliding doors in the front of the piano just over the keyboard. She fitted the long roll on a metal rod inside. Then she sat down and began to pump the pedals with her feet.

As Hannah pumped, the roll began to unwind and little square holes appeared in the paper. Music began to come out of the piano and the keys began to go up and down. Hannah put her hands on the keyboard and made believe she was playing.

"Red sails in the sunset . . ." she sang.

"Oh, my favorite popular song!" said Aunt Becky. "That looks like fun! Can I pump?" She

took her knitting with her and sat next to Hannah on the piano bench. The edge of the red guess-what touched Hannah's knee. "Ooh, does it feel itchy!" she thought. Hannah moved her hands over the keyboard and Aunt Becky pumped the pedals.

"Red sails in the sunset . . ." they sang together. *Click, click, click,* went Aunt Becky's knitting needles.

"I'll bet my Aunt Becky never stops knitting," thought Hannah. "Except to go to sleep or go to the bathroom."

Just as they finished, Aunt Becky gave a big yawn.

"My goodness, I'm still sleepy," she said. "Thank you, Hannah dear. I think I'll go put my bathrobe on and be comfortable."

Hannah rewound the roll and put it back inside the piano bench.

"Did you write your movie letter to Grandma?" asked Hannah's mother.

"Not yet," said Hannah. "But I will later. I have to talk to Daddy." The cash register rang and

Hannah ran out into the restaurant. Her father was just ringing up a dollar bill from the gas customer.

"When'll we take the fish out?" whispered Hannah.

"Now," said her father. Hannah tiptoed into the bathroom behind her father and closed the door. She picked up the little fishnet.

"Wait here a minute," said Hannah's father. "I just got another idea." He opened the trapdoor and went down to the cellar. Hannah waited a minute. Then she put the fishnet down and followed him. She closed the trapdoor quietly. She wanted to make sure her father didn't wake Skippy up.

"He's still asleep," whispered Hannah. "Shh . . ." Her father folded a little piece of paper and stuck it in his pocket.

"Okay. Now I'll race you back up," said Hannah's father. "You take the outside steps and I'll take the inside."

"No fair—you'll win," said Hannah.

"Okay," said her father. "I'll even count to ten before I start and I bet I'll still win."

"Count to *twenty*," said Hannah.

"One, two, three, four, five . . ."

Hannah ran to the cellar door and opened and closed it quietly. She ran up the outside steps and around to the front door of the restaurant. She ran through the restaurant and the kitchen into the living room.

"Why are you running like that?" asked her mother, looking up from her book. "You're all out of breath."

"I'm racing Daddy," said Hannah, puffing.

Hannah ran to the door of the bathroom.

"I beat!" she yelled. But before she could even turn the doorknob, she heard, *"Help! Fish!"* It wasn't her father's voice. It was Aunt Becky's!

Hannah's mother dropped her book and jumped up.

"Gevalt! A head!"

"She's talking Jewish!" Hannah said.

There was a thump and a bang and loud sounds going down to the cellar.

"Becky!" called Hannah's mother, knocking on the bathroom door. "What happened?"

The door to the bathroom opened. Aunt Becky was in her bathrobe with an empty jar in her hands. Pink powder was all over the floor.

"I decided to take a bubble bath!" she said. "I got my jar of bubble bath from my satchel—I went to fill the tub—but the tub is full of little fish! Swimming around! And then a head popped up from the floor, like a jack-in-the-box! A *head*—a *real live head*! It must be a burglar. I got so excited, my jar of bubble bath turned upside down and all the bubble-bath powder fell on the floor!"

"Oh, my goodness!" said Hannah's mother. "Nobody told Becky how to lock the trapdoor when we use the bathroom so no one can come up from the cellar!"

"Trapdoor?" asked Aunt Becky. *"What trapdoor?"*

"Calm yourself, Becky," said Hannah's mother. "There are no burglars—that was your brother Izzie trying to come upstairs! He runs up and down all day long—I can't believe he didn't show you how the trapdoor works! And goldfish in the bath-tub again—Oh, that man! One day I'll pull out the plug and let his fish take a swim down the drain!"

Hannah ran back outdoors. She ran around the side and down the outside steps. She opened the door to the cellar and ran inside.

Her father was standing by his worktable with his hands over his mouth. Pink powder was all over his hair. His face was very red.

"Aunt Becky said 'Help!' twice," said Hannah. "Once in English and once in Jewish: *'Gevalt!'*"

"I heard," said Hannah's father. "When she

screamed, I went down the steps so fast, I almost broke my neck!" He put his hands back over his mouth. His shoulders shook. He made funny sounds. He was *laughing!*

Hannah stood next to her father at his workbench. She started to say, "It isn't nice to laugh," the way she knew her mother would. But before she could say it, Hannah started to laugh too. She put her hands over her mouth like her father. And Hannah and her father laughed and laughed inside their hands.

Skippy came running over. His eyes were shining. His tail was wagging. He jumped up and licked Hannah's hands.

"Skippy! You woke up! You ate all your scraps!" said Hannah. "Good!" Then, "Look," she whispered to her father. "I think Skippy is laughing too!"

Hannah's mother came down to the cellar.

"Shame on you two!" she said. "Is it nice to give someone a scare and then *laugh?*"

"No, it isn't nice," said Hannah. "It's terrible!"

She looked at her father and both of them started to laugh again.

"You have pink hair!" Hannah said to her father.

"The whole bathroom floor is covered with pink powder," said Hannah's mother. "I thought you promised to tell me in advance when you were going to clean your aquarium. Fish in the bathtub without warning again!"

"I mentioned this afternoon I was going to clean it before the judges came," said Hannah's father.

"Not to me you didn't," said Hannah's mother. "It's lucky Becky didn't have a heart attack. She's in Hannah's bed trying to calm herself now. The least you could do is come up and apologize. She's very insulted."

"I didn't know she was in the bathroom," said Hannah's father. "The trapdoor wasn't locked."

"How should she know how to lock the trapdoor when none of us showed her how to use the slide bolt?" asked Hannah's mother. "She didn't even know there *was* a trapdoor."

"It was a mistake," said Hannah's father. "Usually my trapdoor and my inside stairway to the cellar are the first things I show somebody who sees the place for the first time. You know it's my favorite invention. But I was so busy today I didn't have time to give Becky my usual tour. I just forgot."

"After Becky made matzo balls for you and carried them all the way out here from Brooklyn in a jar in her satchel!" said Hannah's mother.

Hannah's father had found a broom and was sweeping pink powder off the indoor cellar stairs. "I'll go up and sweep the bathroom too," he said.

"And get those fish out of the tub," said Hannah's mother.

"I have to go back up now, Skippy," said Hannah. "So I can fish the goldfish out of the bathtub with the little net. But I'll come down later and say good night." She went up the inside steps with her father. Her mother went out the cellar door and up the outside steps.

Hannah's father pushed the trapdoor up and he and Hannah went up into the bathroom. Hannah put the trapdoor down. They looked at the pink floor.

"What a mess!" said Hannah's father.

"It's bubble-bath powder," said Hannah.

"I hope it didn't get on my goldfish!" said her

father. He ran over to the tub and looked in.

"Whew!" he said. "None of it went into the tub. It's all on the floor. That was lucky—I don't know if bubble bath would agree with my goldfish. You can start fishing them out now if you want to, Hannah. I better go in and apologize to Becky before I start sweeping."

"Don't be mad at me, Becky," Hannah heard her father say. "It was just a mistake. I didn't know you were in the bathroom. Remember when we listened to the opera, I told you, wait till you see the aquarium after I give it my monthly cleaning? This was it."

Hannah fished a goldfish out of the bathtub with the little net and lowered it gently into the pail of water. She took out another to keep it company. Then she peeked into her bedroom. Aunt Becky was sitting up in bed. She was knitting again!

"It's a good thing I had a little bit of knitting left to do on this guess-what," Aunt Becky said to Hannah's father. "Knitting is the only thing that calms me when I get excited."

"I'll sweep the bathroom floor and after the fish are back in the aquarium, I'll clean out the tub with Bon Ami," said Hannah's father. "Then I'll show you how we lock the trapdoor and you can still take your bath. A warm bath is very relaxing and calming."

"No, thank you," said Aunt Becky, clicking her needles. "I'd worry maybe one teeny little gold-fish got left over and I was sitting on it. I'll save my bath till tomorrow. Tonight I'll let my knitting relax me and calm me down. Goldfish in the bathtub—a head popping up out of a floor—who ever heard of such things?"

"I'll make cocoa too," said Hannah's father. "Nice hot cocoa is good before bed." He looked up and saw Hannah. "Hannah loves it, don't you?"

"With a marshmallow on top," said Hannah.

Hannah and her father went back to the bath-room. Hannah finished fishing the goldfish out of the bathtub and her father swept the bathroom floor. Hannah helped her father put all the gold-fish back into the aquarium. Her mother went into the bedroom to talk with Aunt Becky.

Then Hannah's father went into the kitchen and made four cups of cocoa. He put a marshmallow on top of Hannah's the way he knew she liked it. They all had their cocoa in Hannah's bedroom to keep Aunt Becky company. Aunt Becky stopped her knitting just long enough to drink her cocoa.

"I do like cocoa," she said.

Hannah waited a minute to let her marshmallow melt into the cocoa. Then she tasted it. "Mmm," she said. "Delicious!"

When they had all finished, Aunt Becky looked at Hannah's father.

"Izzie," she said, "you have pink hair!"

Then everybody laughed, even Hannah's mother.

"Well, I guess we can all go to bed now," said Hannah's mother. "This was a long day."

"In just one minute," said Hannah. "I promised Skippy I'd say good night."

She took her cup and saucer to the kitchen and while her father rinsed the dishes, Hannah got Skippy a marshmallow. She brought it down to the cellar.

"Good night, Skippy!" said Hannah. Skippy jumped up. Hannah gave him a hug and a marshmallow. Then Hannah's father came down the steps.

"More figuring out?" asked Hannah.

"No," said her father. "We forgot something." He looked at Skippy and began to clap.

"Oh!" said Hannah. "You remembered!" She clapped too. She clapped her very best clapping. Skippy thumped his tail on the floor and chewed his marshmallow.

"He *likes* being clapped for," Hannah told her father. "Thanks! See you in the morning, Skippy!"

Hannah and her father went back upstairs. Her mother was using the broom now. She was sweeping footprints off the floor between the bathroom and Hannah's bedroom.

"Oh, how pretty!" said Hannah. "Pink footprints!"

"Save some work for tomorrow," said Hannah's father. "Let's get a little sleep around here. The judges might come tomorrow."

"You and those judges!" said Hannah's mother.

"For all you know, those judges might not come at all!"

Hannah kissed her mother and father good night.

"I hope they do come tomorrow," she whispered to her father. "And I hope you win." She went into her bedroom. Aunt Becky was leaning over from the edge of the bed and putting her knitting into her satchel.

"Enough excitement for one night," said Aunt Becky. "I'll finish the guess-what tomorrow. Do you think you can wait to guess what?"

"Whew!" said Hannah to herself. She was relieved because whenever Aunt Becky finished with a guess-what, she said, "What should I knit next?" and Hannah never knew what to say.

"Sure, Aunt Becky," she said out loud. "I can wait." She put on her pajamas, turned out the light, and jumped into bed. Then she jumped back up, turned the light back on, rolled up the top of her rolltop desk, and took out a pencil and a piece of paper. She sat down at her desk.

"Dear Grandma," she wrote. "I'm too tired to

write about the movie tonight. I'll tell you all about it tomorrow."

She closed the rolltop desk, turned the light off, and got back into bed. Aunt Becky was so quiet, Hannah thought she had fallen asleep already.

"I'm sleepy too," thought Hannah. Her eyelids felt heavy. But all of a sudden Aunt Becky began to sing—again!

"Maybe you thought with all the excitement of the day that your Aunt Becky forgot her promise," Hannah heard. "But I would never break a promise to my Hannah. Especially after she had such a disappointment at the dog show with her jumping dog!" Hannah could feel her face get hot again. "And she missed more than half of the beautiful opera," Aunt Becky continued. "So here it is! This is the story of *Madame Butterfly!*"

Hannah couldn't believe her ears. But Aunt Becky sang and told *the whole story!*

"Once upon a time in Japan," she said, "there was Madame Butterfly, also known as Cio-Cio-San. And there was Pinkerton." She sang and sang.

"Madame Butterfly was so nice," she went on. "Pinkerton started out nice too, in the beginning, but in the end, he turned into a real stinker."

Aunt Becky sang on and on.

"Oh," said Hannah to herself, "this is worse than listening to the opera on the radio when my father has it on full blast! I'm a prisoner in my own bed! There isn't anyplace I can go to to get away!"

So she went to the only place she could think of.

She went to sleep.

And she had a dream.

Hannah's Dream

Click, click, click! and *bubble bubble!* What could be making those sounds? Hannah jumped up.

Click, click, click! She followed the sounds into the living room. Aunt Becky was sitting by the radio. The radio was on very loud.

"Please look in the kitchen to make sure my pot is not boiling over," said Aunt Becky. "If I get up, I'll drop a stitch."

Hannah went into the kitchen. *Bubble, bubble!* Steam was coming out of a great big pot on the stove. The pot was full of Aunt Becky's soup. A hundred giant matzo balls were dancing in the bubbling broth.

"I think I'll eat one," said Hannah. She got a

bowl and ladled out a little soup and one huge matzo ball. She took a bite and got ready to crunch. But it wasn't hard and chewy, the way Hannah liked it. It was soft and fluffy, the kind grown-ups liked.

"Ugh!" said Hannah to herself. "I don't like soft matzo balls. Mushy!" She turned off the stove. "I'll save the other ninety-nine for my mother and father," she thought. "*They* like soft matzo balls."

"And now," said a voice from the radio, "the golden curtain goes up on the Metropolitan Opera of the Air."

Hannah ran back into the living room.

Click, click, click! Aunt Becky was still knitting next to the radio. A long piece of her wool was wrapped around the dial of the radio. Hannah went over to unwind the wool so it wouldn't tangle Aunt Becky's knitting.

"Don't touch that dial!" said Aunt Becky. "If you touch the wool, the music will stop!"

Click, click, click! Click, click, click!

Hannah stared at the radio. She watched Aunt Becky's needles and Aunt Becky's wool.

"I am knitting a surprise," said Aunt Becky. "Guess what."

The guess-what was white. It was getting longer. Besides Aunt Becky's usual lumps and bumps, it had square holes in different places. It looked just like one of the rolls inside Hannah's player piano. Aunt Becky's wool was moving just like the rolls, and music was coming out.

Aunt Becky was *knitting an opera!*

Click, click, click! A man popped out of the roll! He was wearing a knitted white suit—with lumps and bumps!

"Hello," he said to Hannah "My name is Pinkerton. I'm looking for Madame Butterfly." He ran all around the room.

Click, click, click! There was Madame Butterfly! She popped right out of the roll too and ran after Pinkerton. She was wearing a lumpy bumpy knitted kimono.

Pinkerton and Madame Butterfly hugged and kissed each other. Then they began to sing.

"Ooh!" said Pinkerton right in the middle of his song. "This suit is so itchy!" He wiggled around.

Then they sang some more.

"Ooh!" Now Madame Butterfly stopped singing. "My kimono is itchy too!" she said.

Click, click, click! Pinkerton began to change his shape! One minute he was a big handsome man in an itchy white suit. The next minute Pinkerton changed into a giant cigar!

Madame Butterfly began to cry.

"Pinkerton!" she called. "Pinkerton! Where are you?"

"He's inside that cigar!" Hannah tried to call out. But her voice was stuck.

Click, click, click!

"That big stinker!" said Aunt Becky.

Poof! Pinkerton went up in smoke.

Hannah opened the windows to let the smoke out.

Aunt Becky cried into her knitting.

"What a sad love story," she said. She began to sing along with the radio.

Hannah ran out of the living room and down the cellar steps. Skippy ran over and jumped up on Hannah and they danced around in circles till they came to the cellar door. Then they waltzed up the outside steps, across Route 9W, and all the way to the top of the mountain.

"Hey, wait for us!" Hannah heard. It was Aggie and Otto. They danced up the mountain with Hannah and Skippy.

When they got to the top, they heard a rustling sound in the tall grass in front of Hannah's secret place.

"Listen!" said Otto. "Somebody's in there!"

"Maybe it's a burglar!" said Aggie.

"Who's in there?" called Hannah. The tall grass parted and out came the manager of the movies.

"Hey, that's my special place!" said Hannah. "You can't go in there!" She looked at Skippy and pointed to the manager.

"Remove that man from these premises at once!" she said. Skippy chased the manager all the way down the mountain and down to the river road. Hannah, Aggie, and Otto ran behind them.

They came to the river. The manager fell in.

Skippy jumped into the river and saved him. The manager shook himself off.

"That dog just saved my life!" he said. "Give that dog a blue ribbon!"

Suddenly Aggie and Otto were gone, and Aunt Becky appeared with her satchel and her knitting needles. She pulled some blue wool out of the satchel and knitted Skippy a blue ribbon. She tied it around his neck.

"You are one swell dog," she said.

Skippy started to run. Hannah and Aunt Becky chased him. He ran all the way back up to The Grand View Restaurant. Hannah's mother and father were looking up and down the road for them.

"There they are!" said Hannah's mother. "Oh, look at my garden!" Hannah looked through the openings in the latticework fence. Her father had painted half her mother's yellow flowers blue!

"That man!" said Hannah's mother.

"I'm out of paint!" said Hannah's father. "And I have two more shingles left to go on the garage!"

Aunt Becky reached into her satchel for more wool. She knitted one blue, then one yellow shingle. She knitted them onto the garage.

"Now you'll surely win your certificate for Most Attractive Place on Route 9W," she said.

Hannah heard a funny noise outside. It got louder. She ran back out with Skippy.

"All aboard!" she heard. She looked around. Aunt Becky had knitted a little airplane! It was just big enough for two. She had even knitted a little pilot.

"Ready?" asked the pilot. Aunt Becky knitted him a cap and a pair of goggles.

"Ready!" said Aunt Becky.

The motor started. The propeller went round. The airplane took off. It climbed higher and higher till it looked like a bird.

Hannah and Skippy waved as long as they could still see it.

"Hey, take this itchy blue thing off my neck now!" said Skippy. "It's choking me!"

"*Skippy!*" said Hannah. "You can *talk*! Oh, I always wished you could!" She untied the blue ribbon.

"Look!" said Skippy. "Skywriting!"

Hannah looked up. It was *knitted* skywriting!

"It says, SO LONG, HANNAH!" she said to Skippy. "It says more, but I can't see . . ."

"It says, WHAT SHOULD I KNIT NEXT?" said Skippy. "And GOOD LUCK, IZZIE. I HOPE YOU WIN YOUR CERTIFICATE FOR MOST ATTRACTIVE PLACE ON ROUTE 9W."

"*Skippy!*" said Hannah. "You can even *read*! You're the smartest dog I ever saw!"

All of a sudden, Hannah was shaking and jiggling. She opened her eyes. She was in bed. Aunt Becky was shaking her.

"Hannah, darling, wake up," said Aunt Becky. "You were having a dream! You were hollering Skippy can talk and Skippy can read and I hope Izzie should win his certificate for Most Attractive Place on Route 9W!"

Hannah blinked. Then she laughed at her dream.

"Oh, Aunt Becky," she said. "I really do hope my father wins his certificate!"

"Me also, darling," said Aunt Becky. "Now let's go back to sleep."

Plain and Fancy

In the morning, Hannah wrote her grandmother the whole story of the Shirley Temple movie. Then she went down to the cellar to tell Skippy about her dream.

Skippy was standing with his front paws on the edge of the worktable. He was watching Hannah's father paint something. Hannah put her arm around Skippy's neck and watched too.

Her father had made a little sign.

"For the garage door," he explained.

He was painting a border of blue and yellow squares around the edges.

"A perfect match," he said.

Hannah looked at the sign and she looked at Skippy.

"Hey, Skippy!" she said. "I had a dream that you could *read*! But I bet you can't read *that*!" She pointed to the sign.

"PRESIDENT OF THE INDEPENDENT BENEVOLENT GAS DEALERS' ASSOCIATION OF ROCKLAND COUNTY," Hannah read to Skippy. "That's my pop!" Skippy wagged his tail.

"Yoo-hoo, Hannah!" The trapdoor opened. Hannah looked up and saw Aunt Becky looking down.

"See, Izzie," said Aunt Becky. "Now I know how to use the trapdoor too. Mollie showed me. Look, Hannah—your guess-what is finished!" She held up a long wide rectangle. It was *so* long and *so* wide it seemed to fill the whole trapdoor opening. Hannah thought of the big red flag she had seen in a picture in a new library book called *The Story of Ferdinand*. In the picture, a man called a matador had waved the red flag at Ferdinand the bull to try to get him to fight in the bullring. Hannah had liked Ferdinand because he preferred to just sit and smell the flowers. Aunt Becky's guess-what looked just like the red flag, thought Hannah. But Aunt Becky didn't look like the matador.

Hannah went up the inside stairs.

"See you later," she told Skippy and her father.

When Hannah got up into the bathroom, she closed the trapdoor. She and Aunt Becky went into the living room.

Aunt Becky held up the long wide red guess-what. It was full of lumps and bumps.

"Guess what!" she said.

Hannah knew it would hurt Aunt Becky's feelings if she said, "A flag to wave at Ferdinand the bull." So she said, "I give up," instead.

"It's a scarf," said Aunt Becky. "You mean to say you couldn't guess a *scarf*? It's easy!"

"Well—maybe because it's spring," said Hannah. "I didn't see a scarf since wintertime. . . ."

"Listen, Hannah," said Aunt Becky, "seasons come and seasons go before you know it. There's a famous saying that if spring comes, winter isn't far behind. So always be prepared. That's my motto." She folded the width in half. Now it looked less like a flag and more like a scarf, but Hannah had never seen such a long one. Aunt Becky wrapped it around Hannah's neck three times.

"On a freezing cold day in winter, you'll have the warmest neck in Grand View or Nyack," she said. "When I get back home, I'll make you tassels for both ends and send them to you in the mail. Unfortunately I ran out of wool. I think I'll go call up Mrs. Bluestone again and see how my dear little Poopala-darling is doing without me today."

Aunt Becky went out to the restaurant to use the phone booth. Hannah's mother was straightening out the menus at the tables.

"Look!" said Hannah to her mother when Aunt Becky had gone into the phone booth. "A scarf! It's so hot and itchy!"

"Well, of course it's hot on a nice warm day in springtime," said Hannah's mother. "But in winter a thing like that could come in very handy."

"You said that same exact thing once when Aunt Becky sent me a funny-looking red-and-white stocking cap!" said Hannah.

"And *didn't* it come in handy?" asked her mother.

Hannah had to admit it had. She had worn it home on her foot one day when one of her galoshes had got lost in the snow.

"Try to think of something nice to say to Aunt Becky when she comes out of the phone booth," said Hannah's mother. "Her knitting needles are filled with love. And you are her favorite person in this world."

"I know," said Hannah. She unwound the scarf. "Can I help with something in the restaurant? I already wrote my letter to Grandma."

"Then how would you like to help me make up hamburgers?" asked Hannah's mother. "Yesterday when the bus came, I didn't have enough made up. Today I'd like to have a few stacks ready in the refrigerator so I can just take them out and fry them when I need them."

"I hope we don't get any bus today," said Hannah. But she loved making stacks of hamburgers. She liked to use the special new hamburger invention her father had made. She liked it as much as using the soda machine, which her father always said was a wonderful invention too, even though he hadn't made it himself.

"Okay!" said Hannah. "Let's make hamburgers!"

Hannah and her mother went into the kitchen. Her mother took a large package of chopped meat out of the refrigerator and opened it up. Hannah pulled out a drawer under the kitchen table and took out the new hamburger maker her father had invented. She also took out a rolling pin. She put the hamburger maker and the rolling pin on top of the table and closed the drawer. Her mother unrolled a piece of waxed paper and put the chopped meat on top of it. Hannah rolled out the large piece of chopped meat like it was cookie dough. She picked up the big hamburger maker. It was made of strips of wood nailed together. Some went up and down, and some went sideways. The strips crisscrossed each other and made big square openings in between. Hannah brought the hamburger maker down with a bang on the rolled-out chopped meat.

"There!" she said, lifting it up. "Twelve hamburgers with one blow! I like this new hamburger maker even better than the old one!" The old hamburger maker Hannah's father had invented only made nine at a time.

Just then Aunt Becky came into the kitchen She looked at the table.

"What's that?" she asked.

"My father's invention," said Hannah. "It makes a bunch of hamburgers at one time. The only thing is, they come out square instead of round, so the four corners stick out of the hamburger rolls. My father says the customers get four extra bites." Hannah remembered what her mother had told her while Aunt Becky was in the phone booth. She thought a moment. "Red is a very nice color for a scarf, Aunt Becky," she said. "I'll really show up in the snow."

"Thank you, darling," said Aunt Becky. "I'm glad you like it. I love to make people happy." Aunt Becky frowned. "Mrs. Bluestone says my little Poopala-darling is not eating without me. I wish she was here. I'd make her one of those square hamburgers. That's very nice-looking meat. Poopala-darling loves hamburgers."

"And she'd get four extra bites because of the corners," said Hannah.

"I think it's time for me to go home," said Aunt Becky. "If I go home, Poopala-darling will eat again. I don't want my little dog to starve. And also I don't like being without wool."

"But you can't go home without eating lunch," said Hannah's mother. She stacked the hamburgers in a pile with little pieces of waxed paper in between so they wouldn't stick together.

"Well, maybe I would eat a hamburger first, then," said Aunt Becky. "Even though it's a little early for lunch yet."

"Me too," said Hannah. "Let's eat hamburgers on the porch. We could have a picnic at the table with the painted umbrella." Hannah loved picnics because then she could have a bottle of soda. Usually her mother didn't let her have soda with meals because it filled her up too much.

"Go ask your father if he would like a hamburger too," said Hannah's mother. "So I'll know how many to make."

Hannah ran to the bathroom and pulled up the trapdoor.

"We're going to have a picnic lunch on the porch," she called. "You want a hamburger?"

"Not yet," said Hannah's father. "I still have a few extra things to do." Hannah saw he was writing on one of the little pieces of paper she had seen sticking up out of his pockets.

"Oh, he's working on his new surprise again," she thought. She wondered what it was. She put the trapdoor down and ran back to the kitchen. Her mother had put two hamburgers into the frying pan.

"Daddy's not ready yet," said Hannah. "He's still working on things."

Hannah's mother put the rest of the stacked hamburgers on a plate and into the refrigerator.

"Get two sodas for you and Aunt Becky, then," she said. "And set the table for yourselves on the porch."

"Come on, Aunt Becky," said Hannah. "I'll show you how the soda box works."

Aunt Becky went into the restaurant with Hannah.

"What's your favorite flavor?" asked Hannah. "Mine is sarsaparilla."

"I'll take a root beer, thank you, darling," said Aunt Becky.

Hannah took one warm bottle of root beer and one warm bottle of sarsaparilla from the piles of soda under the counter. She told Aunt Becky to feel them. Then she opened a metal flap on the right side of the green-enameled soda box. Under the flap was a row of holes. She pushed the root beer soda into the hole that had root beers. A cold bottle of root beer popped up from under another metal flap on the left side of the soda box.

"Abracadabra!" said Hannah. She handed it to Aunt Becky.

"Cold as ice!" said Aunt Becky. "But when you put it in, it was warm. How did it get cold so fast?"

"It's not the same bottle," explained Hannah. "There's a lot of other bottles in a long tube that goes down and under and up the other side. They're cold from being in there so long because there's a big block of ice inside in the center. It keeps things cold like an icebox. When I push a warm bottle in the right side, a cold one pops up from the left side."

"Amazing!" said Aunt Becky. "You certainly have all the latest of everything at The Grand View Restaurant. It's some swell soda box and some swell place."

Hannah pushed the warm sarsaparilla bottle into the hole for sarsaparillas and took the cold one that popped up out of the other side. She took four straws and gave two to Aunt Becky.

She opened their sodas from an opener on the side of the soda box. Then they took their sodas into the kitchen and Hannah's mother asked her to get her a Coca-Cola.

"I made a hamburger for myself too," she said. "We might as well eat while we can before the lunch customers start."

Hannah went back into the restaurant and pushed a Coca-Cola into the soda box for her mother. She took the cold bottle that popped up out of the other side, opened it, got two more straws, and went through the kitchen and living room onto the porch. The table was set under the painted yellow umbrella, and Hannah sat down and joined her mother and Aunt Becky.

First Hannah bit the four corners off her hamburger and put them on the edge of her plate.

"I always save the corners for Skippy," she explained to Aunt Becky. Then she bit into the hamburger and roll.

"Mmm," she said. "Our hamburgers are *so good!*" She took another bite. "And juicy," she said. She took a sip of her sarsaparilla. Then she looked up and saw a long gray car drive up to the fence between the restaurant and the garage.

"The magic way to make customers come," Hannah's mother told Aunt Becky, "is to sit down and try to eat something yourself."

The doors of the gray car opened. Three people got out and began to walk around and look at things. One was a lady with a fur piece with a fox's nose at the end. The other was a lady holding funny eyeglasses with a handle on one side. The third was a man with the tallest, stiffest white collar Hannah had ever seen.

Hannah opened her mouth, but not to take another bite of hamburger.

"It's not customers," she said. "It's the judges!" She jumped up.

"I have to go tell Daddy," said Hannah. She ran to the bathroom and picked up the trapdoor. She ran down the stairs.

"The *judges* came!" she said to her father. "They're here!"

"The judges!" said Hannah's father. He dropped his pencil. He dropped his papers. He picked up the papers and stuffed them into his pockets.

"Tell them I'll be right up!" he said. "I have to put my sign on the garage door." He picked up the sign. He ran to the door. He ran back to Hannah.

"If I win my certificate for Most Attractive Place on Route 9W, we'll go to Eagle's and get a banana split to celebrate!" he said.

"Eagle's!" said Hannah. "A banana split!" Eagle's was expensive. They usually only went there for a birthday or other really special occasions.

"Oh, boy!" said Hannah. "I'll race you up the steps!"

Her father ran up the outside steps and she ran up the inside steps.

"See you later, Skippy!" Hannah called as she put the trapdoor down. "The judges are here!"

She ran to the restaurant. When she got there, the judges were just coming toward the door. Her mother and Aunt Becky were waiting for them. The lady with the fur piece with the fox's face said something to the lady with the glasses with the handle on one side. They both turned to the man with the big stiff collar and all three of them burst out laughing as they came through the door.

"It must be a good joke," said Hannah's mother.

"It's the outside colors!" said the lady with the fur piece. "The blue and yellow colors. I never saw a checkered building before!"

"Hilarious!" said the lady with the fancy eyeglasses.

"Unbelievable!" said the lady with the fur piece.

"Dreadful!" said the man with the stiff collar.

"'Hilarious?' 'Unbelievable?' 'Dreadful?'" said Hannah to herself. She didn't like those words or the way the judges said them. She was glad she had beat so her father didn't hear.

Just then Hannah's father came running into the restaurant. He was all out of breath. He was very excited. His eyes were shining. His cheeks were pink.

"Well?" he asked the judges. "How do you like my place *this* year? I thought all year of a way to make it more spectacular."

The three judges burst out laughing again.

"Oh, it's a spectacle all right," said the man with the collar.

"It's just too *much* of a spectacle," said the lady with the glasses.

"Too, too much!" said the lady with the fur piece. Hannah didn't like the way the judges were laughing either. It wasn't the kind of laughing she and her father had been doing in the cellar yesterday when they had tried to stop but couldn't. The judges were laughing on purpose.

Hannah stared into the beady eyes of the fox's face at the end of the lady's fur piece. She felt like pinching the fox's nose and snapping it off.

The lady with the glasses went into the kitchen and held her glasses up over her nose and looked through them at everything.

"The place is as clean as ever," she said to the other two judges when she came back into the restaurant. She checked some notes she had written in her little notebook with notes they had written in theirs.

"So we will award the certificate for Cleanest Place on Route 9W again," said the man.

"But I already got that last year," said Hannah's father. He pointed to the framed certificate on the wall. "I was hoping for the certificate for Most Attractive this time. I picked my color scheme from the gas pumps. Then I thought of the checkered shingle idea. I even thought I'd change the Grand View sign on the roof to The Checkerboard. . . ."

Hannah felt funny when her father said that.

"He picked the colors from the gas pumps!" the lady with the fur piece said to the lady with the glasses. They burst out laughing again.

"My brother," said Aunt Becky, "is the president of the Independent Benevolent Gas Dealers' Association. . . ."

The man with the big stiff collar interrupted.

"I'm afraid Most Attractive is out of the question," he said. "Those blue and yellow shingles are just too conspicuous."

"Too *conspicuous?*" asked Hannah's father. "But I thought it was such a good idea—everything matches. . . ."

"Such bourgeois taste," said the lady with the

fur piece to the lady with the glasses.

Hannah wished she had her dictionary.

"Some people like it very much," said Hannah's mother suddenly. She spoke in a clear, firm voice. "Just yesterday," she continued, "three people commented on how much they liked it." Hannah and her father stared at Hannah's mother. "And taste is a matter of opinion," she added. "It's very hard work to paint shingles separate colors like that."

"I'm afraid we have no certificates for hard work," said the man with the stiff collar. He handed Hannah's father a certificate that said Cleanest Place on Route 9W again.

"You'll have to think of something more subdued in the way of a paint job if you want to try for Most Attractive next year," he added.

The judges left. As they went out, Hannah could hear them laughing again.

Hannah's father stared after the long gray car as it drove off.

"They didn't even say good-bye," he said.

"Why should they say good-bye?" asked

Hannah's mother. "They didn't even say *hello*."

"I don't like those judges," Hannah said to herself. "They were *unfriendly*." They reminded her of the mayor's daughter and Coco.

"I can't believe it," said Hannah's father. "Last year he tells me it's too plain and I should make it more spectacular. I spend all year thinking of a way to do it. Now he tells me it's too conspicuous and I should make it more subdued."

"Some people in this world haven't got enough work to do themselves," said Hannah's mother. "So they form committees and go around criticizing the work of other people who do. Who cares about them anyway? Such snooty people. Give me plain people any day."

"But you didn't like it either," said Hannah's father. "How come you changed your mind?"

"I didn't change my mind," said Hannah's mother. "I just said *some* people like it—I didn't say *I* like it. And I said taste is a matter of opinion—because it is."

Hannah was glad her mother had said what she said.

"I *still* like it," said Hannah. "I love it. I think it's beautiful."

"You were one of the three people I had in mind," said Hannah's mother.

"Who are the other two?" asked Hannah's father.

"Becky and Branagan," said Hannah's mother.

"I'm glad you told them how much work it was," said Hannah's father. He leaned against the ice-cream box and set the certificate down. "I didn't think you noticed. So now I have to start all over again and think of a new idea!"

"You don't *have* to," said Hannah's mother. "If you change it again, you'll have to buy more paint. These are hard times. Those judges had a fancy car and fancy clothes . . ."

". . . and they talked such fancy language!" Becky broke in.

"Plain talk is better," said Hannah's mother. "But will the judges pay for new paint?" she asked. "Money doesn't grow on trees!"

"You always say that!" said Hannah. Every time she heard it, it made her wish money *did* grow on trees so she could pick it and put it in the cash register.

"Don't worry," said Hannah's father. "I'll think of something." Hannah knew he would. Her father loved solving problems. Sometimes her mother said she thought Hannah's father made up problems just so he could figure out ways to solve them.

"You still got Cleanest Place on Route 9W," said Hannah.

"Clean is very important in a restaurant," said Hannah's mother. "It's really the most important thing of all. Would you like to eat in a restaurant that wasn't clean?"

"I wouldn't," said Aunt Becky. "It would turn my stomach."

"And you're still the president of the Independent Benevolent Gas Dealers' Association of Rockland County," said Hannah.

"But I wanted to win Most Attractive Place on Route 9W, though," said Hannah's father. "That's what I *really* wanted. When the gas dealers come for our next meeting, I was hoping to show them the new certificate I thought I would win."

"So you'll show them the new Cleanest certificate," said Hannah's mother. She picked up the certificate and handed it to Hannah's father.

Hannah looked at it.

"Does this mean we won't go to Eagle's to get those banana splits?" she asked her father. "Because you said we'd go if you won Most Attractive."

"Is that what I said?" asked Hannah's father. He put the certificate down. "No hurry about framing this," he said. "I already have one—" He was quiet a minute. *"Boy, I could really go for a banana split!"* he said then. "Even if I didn't win the one I wanted."

"Skippy and I didn't win *anything*," said Hannah.

Her father looked at her.

"So why should we miss out on a banana split?" he asked. "Eagle's Ice Cream Parlor is a very nice place to go. The ice cream is homemade and delicious. We could cheer ourselves up."

"And on top of everything else," said Hannah's mother, "those judges had no manners!"

"No manners?" asked Hannah. "But they were so fancy!"

"Fancy is nothing," said Hannah's mother. "*Nothing!* Real manners are just a little consideration for other people's feelings—and that they didn't have. Those stuck-up judges better behave better next year if they want me to let them inside this place again!"

"Hey!" said Hannah. "That reminds me of Skippy!" She ran to the bathroom and opened the trapdoor.

"Skippy!" she yelled, running down the stairs. "We just had some fancy people here—and they had *worse manners than you!*"

Skippy jumped up and licked Hannah's cheek.

"Oh, Skippy!" said Hannah. "You're the friendliest dog I ever met!" She buried her face in his fur. "I just like friendly dogs and friendly people," she whispered.

Banana Splits and Certificates

Hannah ran back up to the restaurant.

Aunt Becky was putting her knitting needles into her satchel.

"Why don't you come to Eagle's too?" Hannah's father asked her mother. "Let's close up for half an hour and we'll all go. I'll make a little sign and leave it on the door."

"Yes, you come too!" said Hannah. "That would be fun. We never get to go anyplace all together. Somebody always has to stay home and mind the restaurant."

"*Me?*" asked Hannah's mother. "I can't eat one of those big banana splits at Eagle's."

"Then get the junior size," said Hannah. "Like I do."

"Thanks," said her mother. "But MelOrols are good enough for me."

Aunt Becky and Hannah's mother hugged each other good-bye. Hannah's father went out and started the car. Hannah turned to follow him. Then she turned back to her mother.

"But your favorite flavor is strawberry," she said. "MelOrols don't even come in strawberry. Just chocolate and vanilla."

"Hannah, don't worry so much," said her mother. "One of these days you'll turn into a worrywart! Go—your father had a big disappointment. Don't keep him waiting. Skippy and I will keep each other company while you're gone."

Hannah ran out and got into the little black car with her father and Aunt Becky.

"Wait'll you see Eagle's Ice Cream Parlor, Aunt Becky," said Hannah. "You'll love it!"

"Thank you, darling, but I really want to catch the next bus back to New York City so I can take the subway to Brooklyn," said Aunt Becky. "I could never eat a banana split while my little Poopala-darling is home starving. I'm in a real hurry to get back so she'll start to eat again."

Hannah's father drove down Broadway until they got to the Nyack bus station.

"The bus is there already," he said. He pulled up to the curb and they all got out. Aunt Becky took her return ticket out of her pocketbook and kissed Hannah and her father good-bye.

"I'll get new wool and make your tassels tomorrow," Aunt Becky told Hannah. Then she bent down and whispered in Hannah's ear, "And I'll make a scarf for your father too. Blue with yellow tassels—or yellow with blue tassels. But don't tell."

"Oh, good, Aunt Becky!" said Hannah. The driver revved up the engine and Aunt Becky got on the bus. She gave her ticket and sat down by a window. She looked out and waved.

"So long, folks!" she called as the bus pulled away from the curb. Hannah and her father waved until they couldn't see Aunt Becky anymore. Then they got back into the little black car and drove to Eagle's Ice Cream Parlor on Main Street.

They sat in a dark wooden mahogany booth with a big beautiful Tiffany light overhead made of all different colored pieces of glass fitted together.

Hannah's father ordered a banana split with one scoop of vanilla, one scoop of chocolate, one scoop of strawberry, a whole banana, strawberry syrup, pineapple syrup, walnuts, whipped cream, and a cherry on top. Hannah knew the price without even looking at the menu: 35¢. She always thought her father was a big spender when he ordered a banana split. Hannah ordered a junior banana split because she knew she could never finish the big expensive size. She ordered one scoop of vanilla, half a banana, strawberry syrup, walnuts, whipped cream, and a cherry on top. That was just the size Hannah liked. She knew that price without looking too: 20¢.

She looked in the mirror beside them and saw the reflections of all the other dark mahogany booths and the glow from the bright-colored

Tiffany lights, and the other people in the other booths just like theirs. All the people in the mirror were talking as they ate. Hannah and her father usually talked a lot too, but now they were quiet. Hannah looked at her father in the mirror. He looked very tired. She kept looking in the mirror till she saw the waitress come with their banana splits and two glasses of ice water.

Hannah took a bite of her vanilla ice cream.

"Mmm," she said. "This homemade ice cream certainly *is* delicious."

They ate slowly and quietly. Suddenly Hannah felt tired too. She put down her spoon and looked straight at her father. She didn't look in the mirror.

"We both lost!" she said.

Her father put down his spoon too and looked straight back at her.

"We got the booby prizes!" he said. He started to laugh.

That made Hannah laugh too. They laughed harder. They laughed until tears came into their eyes. Hannah looked in the mirror and saw the people in the other booths looking at them. She slid down a little in her seat.

"So let's enjoy ourselves!" said her father.

And they picked up their spoons and finished their banana splits.

"I'm getting an idea," said Hannah's father. "In the middle of my banana split, I thought how I could make a new paint job and still save paint.

I'll only need half as much as a whole new job: I'll just paint yellow over the blue shingles. That will be only half of them. The other half are yellow already. So the whole place will be one color, yellow, and it will only cost half as much as a whole new job. And I have another idea: What is yellow?"

"I don't know," said Hannah. She looked down at her father's dish. There was a little pineapple syrup left in the bottom.

"Pineapples?" she asked.

"The sun!" said Hannah's father. "The *sun* is yellow. And what does the sun do? It shines and makes flowers grow. I'll make flower boxes under the windows in front. I'll plant all-color zinnias in the flower boxes. And I'll even *paint* little flowers growing all around the bottom edges of the building—so there'll even be flowers in winter! Then the place will be spectacular but not too spectacular. And it won't be conspicuous but more subdued. But it won't be plain like last year. And I'll change the name to The Flower Box!"

Hannah stared at her father.

"It sounds even more beautiful than the blue and yellow checkers," she said. "And I'd like to help you paint the flowers around the bottom edges. But please—*don't change the name!* When you were going to change the sign on the roof to The Checkerboard, I was worried. I love The Grand View Restaurant. It's still The Grand View Restaurant whatever color or design you make. So don't change the name—okay?"

"*Okay!*" said Hannah's father. He didn't look tired anymore. He put down a big tip for the waitress and Hannah said, "Wow!" And when they paid the bill, he got half a pint of strawberry ice cream to take home in a little white box.

"A surprise for Mother," he said.

"Oh, good!" said Hannah.

"Look what a little pleasure like a banana split can do," said Hannah's father on the way home. "A person can start all new plans."

Hannah didn't think a banana split was a little pleasure. She thought it was a big one.

"I'm glad you got Mother the strawberry surprise," she said. "What's the surprise you're planning on those pieces of paper sticking out of your pockets?" she asked. "Please tell!"

"I usually never tell a surprise before it's made," said Hannah's father, "because then it isn't a surprise anymore—you know. But I'll make an exception just this once—I'll tell you: It's something I know you want. When Mother told me what happened at the dog show yesterday, I decided to make it for you as a surprise. It's a doghouse for Skippy!"

"A doghouse for Skippy!" said Hannah. "Oh, hooray! Now he won't have to stay down in the cellar when he jumps up on people! He can just go in his doghouse instead! Make it look like The Grand View Restaurant—like you did when you made the birdhouse in Mother's garden."

"That's just what I'm planning to do," said Hannah's father. "It will have a real roof and a piece of linoleum on the floor and a little side porch in case he wants to get fresh air or take a sunbath. The outside will have real shingles . . ."

"And make the shingles blue and yellow!" said Hannah. "Just to remember the checkerboard idea by. Skippy won't think it's too conspicuous—he'll love it!"

"Hey!" said Hannah's father. "That's perfect!" He turned in to The Grand View Restaurant and parked the car by the latticework fence. Hannah's mother was poking in the ground in her garden behind the fence. She had let Skippy up from the cellar. Skippy was watching her.

"It's a good thing I didn't go," said Hannah's mother. "I had a lot of lunch customers."

When Skippy saw Hannah, he ran over to the outside steps and up the steps to the gate.

"Skippy!" yelled Hannah. She opened the gate so he could come through. "You're going to get a doghouse! It's a surprise!"

Hannah's father began telling his new paint plans to Hannah's mother over the fence. Hannah ran into the restaurant with Skippy behind her. She went over to the ice-cream box. The new Cleanest Place on Route 9W certificate was still lying on top of it. Hannah picked it up. She opened the ice-cream box and put the small white container from Eagle's on top of the MelOrols.

"That's a little surprise for my mother," she said to Skippy. "The big surprise is for *you*. Aren't you *lucky*?" She closed the ice-cream box and put the certificate back down. She looked at it again.

"Hey—*I've* got an idea for a surprise too!" she said to Skippy. She ran to her bedroom. Skippy ran after her.

"Wait till you see, Skippy!" said Hannah. She rolled up the top of her rolltop desk and sat down. She took a box of crayons out of one of the cubbyholes. She took a piece of drawing paper out of one of the drawers. Then she picked up her pencil. Skippy sat on the floor next to her and thumped his tail on the floor.

Hannah made a row of capital letters on the drawing paper with the pencil. She took a blue and a yellow crayon out of the crayon box and went over the letters carefully, first a blue letter, then a yellow, then a blue, then a yellow, till she had finished. Then she took out all the other colors in the box and made a border of tiny flowers all around the four edges of the paper.

"Come on, Skippy!" said Hannah. She took the

drawing paper and left everything else on the desk. She didn't even wait to close the drawer or the rolltop. She ran back out of her bedroom, through the living room and kitchen and restaurant, out the door, and around to the side of the building.

Her father was waving his hands and talking excitedly to her mother over the fence.

"So just as soon as I finish the house for the dog," he said, "I'll buy just one new gallon of yellow paint, and I'll only have to do *half* a paint job, so it will cost only half as much . . ."

Hannah stuck the piece of drawing paper in her father's hand right in the middle of his sentence.

"Surprise!" she said.

Hannah's father looked at the paper. He stopped talking. It was very quiet for a moment. Then he smiled.

"Hey—look at this!" he said to Hannah's mother. He held it up. Hannah's mother looked up from her garden. Then *she* smiled.

"Now, *that's* what I call a certificate!" she said.

"Read it out loud so Skippy can hear it," said Hannah.

Hannah's father cleared his throat.

"BEST FATHER ON ROUTE 9W," he said. His voice was proud. "I'm going to *frame* that—this minute!"

"Come on, Skippy," said Hannah. "I'll race you up the mountain!"